FRENCH COUNTRY FRIGHTS

/ / / /

J.R. RAIN
&
H.P MALLORY

HAVEN HOLLOW SERIES

Published by
Crop Circle Books
212 Third Crater, Moon

Printed in the United States of America.

ISBN-9798497514551

Chapter One

"Oh, just pick someone already, Fifi," Bea groaned. "They're all cute. Any one of them will do."

"I'm not so sure."

"They're men, not puppies."

I laughed to myself, glancing sideways at the men who populated the run-down bar around us. If you lived in Haven Hollow, usually you frequented The Half-Moon Bar and Grill but because I used to work there, I was over the place and then some. So, tonight, Bea and I had opted to visit The Black Bat which was located in a town just south of the Hollow, called Ashington.

I attempted to buy myself time by picking up my drink and sipping at it as I tried to figure out which one of the men was my favorite. It didn't take long before I figured out none of them were. And that wasn't due to the fact that I was fiercely independent or a man-hater. No, I was probably the biggest romantic I knew—all I really wanted in life was a man who loved me for the real me (and not my succubus powers of attraction), a house with a white picket fence and a couple of kids. Oh, and I wanted my new business, Hallowed Homes, to be successful.

As to my night out with my good friend Bea, I wasn't sure why I'd even let her talk me into this little errand in the first place. It wasn't like she was my wingman, er... wing woman. She was my employee and she'd become one of my closest friends.

Either way, Bea had taken note of how exhausted I was looking lately. It wasn't much of a stretch for her to figure out why—I wasn't feeding. It had been so long since the last time I'd had sex, I could barely even remember it. And, as a succubus, sex should have been at the top of my list. But, I wasn't like other succubae. I wasn't looking for one-night stands or crazy sex that lasted all night long. I was looking for something meaningful, something real. I was looking for forever, even though 'forever' seemed like pie in the sky because I was also completely hopeless when it came to men.

Regardless, I'd let Bea talk me into coming out for drinks this evening and everyone knew 'going out for drinks' also meant cruising the male population. But, none of these guys were really doing it for me, which didn't seem to matter much to Bea. In general, she could be a bit zealous in her easy assessment of things, including which man I should scoop out of the bar, but she meant well.

"I'm not... really into any of them," I answered on a sigh.

"It's not like this is a long-term commitment, Fifi," Bea argued, shaking her head as her Shirley Temple curls bounced around her head. Even though Bea was in her forties, like me, she looked like she was going on twelve with her huge, round green eyes, pert little nose and big smile. Bea was a faerie and she was small, standing only four and a half feet tall. But, her diminutive stature was deceiving. Bea might have been small and slim, but she packed a mean punch, provided by faerie power. Her hair was as fine as the fluff on a dandelion and the same color, though it was always hidden by a hat. Bea liked hats because they concealed her pointed ears from the public (the supernatural community in Haven Hollow was distinctly separate from the human community and we had to keep things that way). Her outfits were equally creative, all of them designed to cover her wings.

Today she wore a frock dress in the colors of the Spring Court, to which she belonged—pastel pink, mint green and bright yellow. The Fae were separated into four courts—each taking its namesake from the seasons. And the easiest way to recognize which court a faerie, pixie, elf or other fae creature represented was to look at the colors they wore. The Autumn Court was fond of earth tones—deep browns, hunter greens, tans and beiges. The Winter Court would usually dress in icy blues, whites, and aquas. The Spring Court and the Summer Courts were the most difficult to tell apart because both wore pastels.

"And yet a long-term commitment is exactly what I'm looking for," I said as I glanced around the room again before bringing my gaze back to my friend. "I'm fairly sure I'm not going to find that 'long-term commitment' here."

"Taking one of these guys home doesn't mean you have to keep him, Fifi," Bea prattled on. "You can keep him for a night and then release him back into the wild tomorrow morning. You don't even have to feed him before you kick him out," she continued with a little, bell-like laugh. It was one of my favorite things about Bea—whenever she laughed, it made me want to laugh.

"The idea is not for you to feed him, but for *him* to feed *you*," she added with a playful wink.

Still, I wasn't interested in one-night stands, especially when a one-night stand wouldn't get me very far. I'd never be able to let down my guard and truly enjoy myself with a human sex partner because a human man would never be able to withstand my feeding from him.

It wasn't like I was a vampire and would bleed a man dry or anything like that. As a succubus, I fed on life force—which might sound just as bad and maybe it was. Regardless, human men didn't possess the stamina required for a true succubus feeding. So, I couldn't feed from a human fully, but I could feed from him enough to take care of the bags under my eyes.

I let out a loud sigh, my shoulders slumping in defeat. Looking around the bar, I could see a number of eyes on me—but that wasn't anything out of the ordinary. I was used to men's attention. Given what I was, a sex demoness, men stared at me all the time with longing, hungry expressions. Lately, the attention I'd been getting from the opposite sex was a bit diminished, owing to a repelling potion Poppy had made for me that dampened my sexual attractiveness. No, men didn't find me repulsive (because Poppy made the potion a weak one), but they also didn't flock to me like they normally would. The potion simply negated the power of my succubus pheromones and put me on the same playing field as any other woman with decent looks. Men still might be attracted to me on a superficial level, but at least that attraction was just a natural appreciation and not uncontrollable lust driving them to be with me. I could still accomplish that uncontrollable lust if I wanted to, but now I was in the driver's seat where my abilities were concerned. For the first time ever, *I* could choose when and where to unleash the true power of my sex appeal rather than having it hovering around me like a constant and unreasonable, passion-pink sex aura.

"I just don't know if I'm ready for all this," I continued on another sigh. "My last boyfriend was a real slug."

"Not all men are slugs, Fifi," Bea argued, in her sing-song voice. Bea was the eternal optimist and sometimes it was hard to be around her. Especially when lately my optimism was pretty much nowhere to be found.

"That might be true," I answered as an image of Marty Zach dropped inside my mind's eye. Marty was a human, but he was immune to the powers of the supernatural. And he was also the perfect man in my perception—humble, kind, handsome and good-hearted. He was everything I wanted in a man, but the sad truth was… I didn't think he thought of me as anything other than a friend. At least, he'd never really given me any indication that he thought of me as anything but.

And, no, I wouldn't have been able to fully feed from Marty. Even though he was a 'null' and couldn't be swayed by the powers of the supernatural, he was still just a human.

"Besides, the realty office needs all of my focus," I continued. "I want Hallowed Homes not only to be successful, but spectacular," I finished, feeling pensive for a moment as my eyes drifted toward the wood on the bar, my thoughts bouncing between excitement over recently opening Hallowed Homes Realty and Marty's blue eyes.

"So, you won't even try?"

I swallowed hard as I looked at her. "I sort of… kind

of… have a crush on someone already, actually." Then I laughed at my own embarrassment.

Bea's enormous grin returned and she leaned in closer. "That's great! Who?"

"I don't want to jinx it by saying."

It was Bea's turn to laugh. "Jinx it? Are we in high school now?" I shook my head as she continued. "Tell me who you have your eye on!"

"Fine!" I answered as I felt heat overcoming my cheeks. "It's um… It's Marty, okay?"

Bea's eyebrows reached for the ceiling as a look of surprise claimed her features. She didn't respond right away but just frowned. "Marty, Marty, Marty," she repeated his name, as if doing so would bring an image of him to mind. "Wait… you mean *Marty Zach*?"

"Right." As far as I knew, there was only one Marty in Haven Hollow.

"The ghost-chaser guy?"

I nodded.

"The one who drives Lorcan around during the day in that black hearse?"

"Yup."

Bea shrugged, but still held onto her shocked expression, even if it was more resigned now. "Well, I didn't see that one coming, but okay... Is he into you, too?"

I shook my head. "No. I mean… I don't think so."

"Are you sure?" Bea asked, frowning at me again. "I mean, how could he *not* be into you?"

I shook my head at her. "Bea, there are plenty of men who aren't into me."

"Um… I doubt that's true. Have you seen yourself?"

I gave her a quick smile for the compliment. "I'm pretty sure Marty doesn't think of me as anything other than a friend."

"Did he say that?"

"Well, no, but it's the feeling I get."

"Hmm," she answered because she was one of those people who strongly believed in listening to one's intuition.

"It just sucks because… Marty is pretty much the nicest guy in Haven Hollow, and he's exactly what I'm looking for. Doesn't that just figure?" I asked on another laugh, tipping my drink back and emptying the contents down my throat in an attempt to soothe the depression that was already creeping back over me.

"Doesn't *what* just figure?"

"That I find someone who's the perfect guy to settle down with and he isn't the slightest bit interested in me."

"Well, first of all, we don't know whether that's even true. He *might* like you."

"Let's just assume he doesn't."

"Well, then… you know what they say. 'If you can't be with the one you love, love the one you're with.'"

"That doesn't help me either because I'm not with anyone," I answered, shrugging as I called the bartender over and ordered another Long Island Iced Tea. "And, besides, that's a dumb comment."

"Don't take everything so literally, Fifi. What I'm saying is that if Marty isn't interested in you the way you wish he were, you should forget him and find someone who is. Someone to get your freak on with."

"I don't want to get my freak on with anyone!"

"You might not want to, but you *need* to. Your body needs to." I couldn't argue with her there. Because I hadn't fed properly in the last five years, I hadn't felt fully healthy in the last five years either. Instead, I was prisoner to a constant sense of fatigue. Yes, that fatigue lifted for brief moments when I was able to feed from a man while kissing him or the like. During those brief moments, I was able to absorb some of his life force, but those impromptu feedings still weren't enough. And there was always the threat that the succubus within me would overpower my reasoning and logic mind and suck a man dry.

"If you feed, Fifi, it will improve your focus and you'll feel better," Bea continued, giving me an expression of pity. "You look like you haven't slept in two weeks."

"It's just… not that simple."

"It *is* that simple," she argued. "You pick a guy from this bar, take him home, get your rocks off, and you kick him out the next morning. Hell, you can kick him out when you're done if you want. No strings, no regrets."

"It's… too dangerous."

She waved away my concern with her small hand and then took another sip of her spiked cherry lime-aid. "Please tell me you've at least given up trying to divorce your succubus side?"

I swallowed hard because it was a subject that left me cold. I'd told Bea about it, only because I trusted her. There was a time, not long ago, when I'd contemplated visiting a witch who practiced black magic because she'd told me she would be able to separate me from the succubus side of me. Poppy and Wanda had done their best to talk me out of it and they'd succeeded, but only because Poppy had been able to come up with the repelling potion that had basically changed my life.

"Yes, I've given up trying to separate my succubus side," I answered, embarrassed I'd even contemplated it in the first place. Looking back at it, that decision could have been fatal. Now, even though I didn't like my succubus nature any more than I did back then, I also had accepted the fact that I couldn't change what I was. No, but I could… *curb* it.

"Thank Tatiana for that," Bea said, mentioning the name of the fairie Queen of the Spring Court. "And what's the deal with Angelo? Is he still living with you?"

I groaned as I thought about my brother. Angelo was an incubus and although demons were supposed to have tight family connections, my brother and I were anything but. Recently, he'd done his best to ruin me by trying to prove to our parents that I wasn't feeding and therefore, not representing my family name with dignity.

Angelo was hot-headed, selfish, rude, impulsive and the quintessential womanizer. And he was also sharing my house with me at the moment, something I was less than thrilled about. "Yes, he's still living with me."

Bea shook her head. She couldn't stand Angelo and wasn't shy about it. "I swear you let that awful brother of yours walk all over you, Fifi."

"I have responsibilities to my family," I answered. "And loyalty is one of them."

"Yet, he shows you no loyalty at all!" she responded, her eyebrows knotting in the center of her face.

"Well, that's just how Angelo is…" I knew I was making excuses for him, but he *was* my brother and I always hoped things would get better between us. "At least, he won't be staying with me much longer." Angelo was in the middle of replacing all the floors in his house and needed somewhere to live for a couple of weeks while the floors were going down. Why in the world he'd wanted to stay with me was anyone's guess, but when he'd asked, I hadn't turned him down.

"I can't think about your brother because it ruins my

good mood," Bea answered as she spotted a group of men when they laughed loudly. They were sitting at a table near the fireplace at the far end of the bar.

Before I knew what she was doing, she seized my hand and pulled me off the bar stool. She was surprisingly strong for such a little thing. Then she marched over toward the group of guys and I felt my cheeks heat up as a few of them turned to look at us. There were six of them, three with their backs turned to us. As we drew closer, I noticed there was a girl sitting between two of the guys on the backside of the table, but she was looking down at her hands so I couldn't see her face.

"Hey, guys," Bea said as she gave them all a big smile. "Have you met my friend, Fifi?"

Chapter Two

"Hi," the men answered in unison as I felt my cheeks continue to burn. This was just so... embarrassing.

The lively conversation they were having died abruptly as soon as they made eye contact with me, four of the six taking a quick interest, by the looks of it. That was when I remembered I'd forgotten to anoint myself with my repelling potion this morning. That meant my pheromones were stronger than usual. Shoot.

Rather than paying the guys any attention, though, my focus was drawn back to the girl. She looked completely dazed—her eyes unfocused and when she spoke, her words didn't make any sense. She also seemed to be having a tough time just sitting upright. Maybe she was drunk, but I didn't think so.

"Is your friend okay?" I asked, nodding toward her.

"Yeah, she's fine. Too much wine," one of the guys replied immediately—a little too quickly, as though he didn't want her to try to answer for herself.

"Hmm," I said with healthy suspicion. Not taking the guy's word, I continued to look at the woman. She didn't look back at me, so I had to reach out to get her attention and lightly touch her shoulder. "Are you okay?"

Bea was quiet now, her determination to get me laid forgotten as she too began to take an interest in what was going on with this woman. The girl didn't respond, but she did finally look up at me. And when she did, I definitely ruled alcohol out. This didn't look like inebriation, instead, her eyes were hollow and unfocused, as if she were looking through me—as if she couldn't see me. And when she glanced around herself, it appeared she had no sense of her surroundings. Whatever was going on with her was a lot more than too much wine.

"She's fine," one of the men growled, making the hairs on the back of my neck stand up. There was something threatening in his voice, an unspoken warning to mind my own business. He obviously didn't know who he was dealing with, or *what* he was dealing with.

If he thought I was going to leave a vulnerable woman, in her present condition, with a bunch of men I didn't know, he had another think coming.

"Do you want to get some air?" I asked the girl, continuing to ignore the men.

"Mind your own business," the same man said in an even more menacing tone. He turned to face me squarely.

"Yes," the girl barked back, suddenly coming to life. When she looked up at me this time, there was some semblance of coherence in her gaze. "Please," she continued, nodding repeatedly. "I... I need some air." The words sounded like they were coming out in slow motion, almost like she'd had a stroke and her mouth wouldn't work properly.

"Come on," I said as I reached down and took her arm, helping her to stand, which wasn't easy considering she was sandwiched between the two large men. "Let's go outside and hopefully you'll feel better."

"What the hell do you think you're doing?" One of the men barked, glaring at me as he stood up and towered over me.

"Our friend is fine. Like we said, she just had too much to drink," the man on the other side of her added, standing up to reveal his equally large stature, as if to intimidate me. But, I didn't easily intimidate.

The bigger they are, the harder they fall, I thought.

"Oh, yeah?" I asked. "What's your friend's name?"

The guy swallowed hard because he clearly didn't have an answer for me, just like I'd known he wouldn't. If I had to bet, he'd only met this woman in the last couple of hours and had promptly spiked her drink with whatever substance was now making her so loopy.

I gave him a glare and then walked around the table, pulling out her chair so she could bypass both men. She held onto me as if for dear life as I helped her take a few wobbly steps. Bea joined me, balancing the woman on her other side as we began to walk away from the table, toward the back entrance of the room. Another of the men stood and started to follow us as we talked quietly to the woman, attempting to determine what had happened to her and if she was concerned about the men she was with. For all we knew, she'd been roofied.

"My... name is... Alice," the girl managed.

"Okay, Alice, if you're in trouble or if you just want to go home, we can take you," I told her.

"Hey, this doesn't concern you," the large guy who stood up first yelled as he gripped my shoulder, none too gently.

13

"Don't touch me," I growled at him as I released Alice and Bea did her best to keep Alice upright.

"Mind your own business," the man answered, not making any motion to release me.

"You go back and *mind your business!*" I responded through gritted teeth.

The unfortunate part of the whole situation was that if this guy decided to get physical with me, I wasn't at my best since I hadn't fed in too long. Sure, I was still stronger and more powerful than any human on his best day, but I would've been much more powerful if I'd fed.

I managed to shrug out of his hold and giving him one more warning glare, turned to face Bea and Alice. Taking Alice between us again, the three of us stepped onto the sidewalk that ran between the bar and the street. Two of the men followed us. From my peripheral vision, I saw the quick glance between the two of them and knew what was coming next, steeling myself for an attack. Bea apparently noticed it too, and released Alice, looping her arms around a nearby streetlamp. No sooner had Bea released Alice, then the two men charged us, their expressions full of venom. No doubt they thought Bea and I were easy targets, but that's where they were wrong.

Bea launched herself upward, her wings shooting out from her cotton-candy pink dress as she hovered overhead for only seconds before dive bombing the first guy. She may have been tiny, but like most fae, she was powerful and then some. I squared off against the other guy, who was only slightly larger than the first, sidestepping his attempt to land a punch to my cheek. I was quick, but not quick enough and his blow impacted me on my shoulder, throwing my balance off.

"Now you're pissing me off," I ground out, getting

my feet back underneath me as I rushed forward to grab him by the shoulders. He couldn't break my hold and was forced to face me, his eyes going wide as he witnessed the strength in my grip. But, before he could figure out what I was doing, I yanked him down and stepped up onto my tiptoes, pulling him into a kiss. There were two reasons for that—first, to take him by surprise and in taking him by surprise, to disarm him. Second—to boost my own strength by stealing some of his.

He appeared confused for a moment and then his male side kicked in and he immediately kissed me back, wrapping his arms around me as he pulled me in closer, clearly oblivious to what was happening to him. He grabbed each side of my face with his mitt-like hands and thrust his sour-tasting tongue into my mouth, which immediately made me want to heave up my dinner and drinks.

I was so disgusted and angry, I was tempted to drain him of all his life energy, right then and there. But I kept my inner demon under control and decided against it. Instead, I released him, only having absorbed enough of his energy to make him feel like he'd gotten hit with a strong flu, which, in turn, bolstered my own strength.

Stunned and now weak, he dropped to the sidewalk, onto his hands and knees, and looked up at me with a frightened expression. When his friend collapsed beside him, out cold, thanks to Bea, his eyes only went wider.

"What are you?" he managed.

"Someone who won't allow you to take advantage of innocent women," I answered.

Looking toward the back door of the bar, I worried we might have eavesdroppers. But, I was relieved to find we didn't. The rest of the men had remained inside, which was just as well. But Alice was now wandering down the sidewalk, weaving back and forth and looking like she wasn't going to remain upright for very much longer.

"I'll get her," Bea said, taking off in Alice's direction and grabbing her arm to steady her. I caught up to them and helped Bea hold her up as Alice looked at both of us and smiled halfheartedly, clearly still completely out of it.

It was clear that we had to take her to the hospital, but it wasn't a good idea for Bea or me to step foot inside a human hospital—there would be too many questions. And we definitely didn't want to have to deal with the police. But we could drive Alice there, all the same.

"Alice, we need to take you to a hospital. Is there someone you know and trust who can meet us there?" I asked.

"Yesh," she answered, her voice sounding slurred.

"My shister," she finished, looking like she was about to pass out at any moment.

"Okay, that's good."

"Do you have a phone on you, Alice?" Bea asked.

Alice nodded and began fishing around in her wallet-purse which I noticed was strapped around her body, messenger bag style. And, good thing too, because if the purse hadn't been strapped to her, no doubt it would have remained back at the table with those jerks. Before long, Alice produced a large phone in a pink silicone case, complete with bunny ears.

"What's your sister's name?" I asked.

"Joanne," she answered, a little giggle escaping her.

"Okay," I said and scanned through her phone until I found the name "Joanne." Then I called the number and a woman answered.

"Alice?"

"Is this Joanne?" I asked.

"Um, yeah. Who's this and why do you have my sister's phone?"

"My name is Fifi," I answered. "And I'm in Ashington at the Black Bat bar. I'm with your sister and I'm pretty sure she's been roofied by the guys she was with and we're going to take her to the hospital here, in town."

"Oh, God."

"Can you meet us outside the hospital and admit her yourself, since you'll be able to answer their questions better than we can?"

"Yes, I'm actually a nurse and I work at the Urgent Care here in town. We don't have a hospital in Ashington."

"Okay, perfect. What's the address?"

"74 Boons Ferry Avenue. I'll be outside waiting for her. Thank you," she said as her voice cracked. "Thank you so much."

I hung up the phone and put it back in Alice's purse. "Alice, do you know the names of the men you were with?" I asked, hoping the answer was 'yes' so she could press charges against them. She nodded, then shook her head and appeared confused again. I looked at Bea and she nodded.

"I'll go in and swipe their identification," Bea answered my unasked question. What she meant was that she could move incredibly quickly—so much so that she wouldn't be spotted by the human eye. And that meant she could swipe the men's identification without anyone being the wiser. Bea disappeared a second later and I returned my attention to Alice. She was completely out of it and I wondered if she'd even stay conscious for much longer. I was likely the only thing keeping her from collapsing into a heap on the sidewalk at this point.

"I can't believe those douche bags did this to her," Bea said, when she returned, handing me a handful of drivers' licenses. "She's lucky we were there to help her."

I accepted the licenses and unzipping Alice's purse, placed them inside. "Give these IDs to the police, Alice," I said. Alice just looked at me and nodded dumbly.

I had a half a mind to go back into the Black Bat and teach those men a lesson they soon wouldn't forget, but I had Alice to worry about and her safety was top priority. So, the police would have to take care of the rest.

"Let's get her to my car and back to her sister," I said as Bea nodded.

"Shoo are you?" Alice asked, her words slurred and barely audible as she looked at Bea through half-open eyes.

"Your knights in shining armor," Bea answered as I gave her a smile, because I kind of liked the title.

"Oh," Alice said, glancing at me. "You're sho prrrettyyy."

"Thanks," I managed as we reached my Toyota 4Runner and I immediately unlocked it as we both helped Alice into the back seat.

Bea and I climbed into the front seats of the 4Runner, and once I started the engine, Bea looked over at me. "Well, this night didn't go as I'd planned."

"Nope, but I can't say I'm disappointed." I glanced into the rear view mirror as I pulled into the empty street and noticed Alice was now singing something as her eyes wandered around the interior of the SUV. At least she was still awake.

Bea smiled while she entered the address for the Urgent Care into her phone and the directions started pouring out in a woman's voice, complete with an English accent.

"Maybe we should make this our side gig?" Bea asked.

I laughed and shook my head, glancing over at her quickly. "What, like becoming superhero crime-busters?"

She nodded. "All we need are some masks and capes and maybe… name tags."

"Name tags?"

She giggled. "Yeah, I can be 'Crime Busting Bea' and you can be 'Ferocious Fifi'."

I shook my head again. "I'm not sure I like my title."

"'Fear-Killing Fifi'?"

I laughed. "Why don't we both just stick to being really good realtors?"

Chapter Three

I was proud of the changes I'd made to what was once Hallowed Realty and was now Hallowed Homes. The old gray cubicles and generic art were gone. In their place was a spacious, open floor plan, decorated with colorful paintings of Haven Hollow landmarks that really livened up the place. Upon entering, you'd find yourself viewing a painting of the old Courthouse that dated back to the early 1800s. Down the hall was a painting of the wooden covered bridge that led to Haven Park (also known as Cemetery Bridge). On the opposite wall was the town center of Haven Hollow and at the end of the hall was Tayir Mansion.

Hallowed Homes might have been in the macabre business of selling homes to monsters (and some humans), but our office didn't have to look like a Vincent Price movie set.

My old boss, Ophelia, had preferred the drab confines of Hallowed Realty. She'd said blandness in decoration kept the focus on the properties instead of the decor, but I wanted to foster a friendlier environment for my employees and customers. I didn't like how Ophelia had kept us all isolated—separated by our cubicles, into squares of despair. She'd wanted to inspire competition among us, not camaraderie or teamwork. It was every man or woman for themselves, each of us at one another's throats.

It wasn't surprising that Ophelia liked things that way. Ophelia was a night hag, after all. That meant she thrived on chaos, enjoyed causing all the misery she could create. In fact, she fed off it, finding joy in others' pain.

Now that she was gone (done away with by Wanda, the Blood Witch), I planned to do things differently. I preferred to provide my employees with incentives to sell, rather than relying on fear to motivate them. I wanted everyone who worked for me to be happy—to really feel like they could make a name for themselves at Hallowed Homes.

I used to be one of those who slaved away for Ophelia, terrified of what failure might mean if I displeased her. And I'd had more than my fair share of punishment, because Ophelia had considered me a constant screw up. She'd always compared me to my brother, who was a very successful realtor (mainly owing to the fact that he used his incubus powers of seduction on his clients). In Ophelia's mind, I should have followed my brother's example—I should have used my powers as a succubus to entice our male clients into doing exactly what Ophelia wanted them to do.

Sure, I could have gotten what I wanted from them too, eliminating any competition within the office, but I just didn't have it in me to ruin the lives of mostly married men who had no control over themselves when under my power. It wasn't fair or right in my book.

With Ophelia gone (she was now a stone statue that

stood in front of Wanda's duplex), I'd already made numerous changes to the Hallowed Homes building and those changes went beyond just decor. Aside from my brother, my staff still included some of the old guard from Ophelia's brutal reign, such as Glenn, a recently widowed werewolf and a Beta in the local pack. Ivan was a Romanian dragon shifter and then there was Willow, a dryad who embraced her love of trees by landscaping many of our properties. Willow had been instrumental when Ophelia owned the realty office because Ophelia had a… *negative* effect on anything living. The last of the leftovers from Ophelia's time was Ramona, a wraith.

Ramona was over six feet tall, pale, and unbelievably thin. No one could be sure of her age, but she appeared to be around sixty, with blue-gray hair and permanent dark circles beneath her eyes. She was a chain smoker and actually resembled a living cigarette. In her wraith form, Ramona became a shadow being and was terrifying. Well, at least that's what I'd heard about wraiths. I'd never actually seen one and hopefully wouldn't ever see Ramona in her wraith form. As I understood it, a wraith only took their true form when feeling threatened or if they had nefarious actions in mind. Luckily, Ramona was every inch the quiet and retiring old lady type, so I didn't imagine any of us would ever have to come up against her shadow side.

Truth be told, I was surprised Ramona had stayed on after Ophelia died because the two of them had been friends… well, as friendly as someone could be with Ophēlia. Night hags aren't exactly known for being sociable or pleasant. But, surprising though it was, Ramona had stayed on and as far as I could tell, she was happy to still have her position.

Then there were the new hires... Bumblebee (Bea for short) was a faerie from the Spring Court, and she was my closest friend. My most recent hire (whom I'd hired only a few days ago) was Elizabeth Blackburn, who went by 'Libby'. Wanda had raised Libby as a zombie and Libby was still very much stuck in a 1950's mindset. The only reason Libby had come to me, looking for a job, was owing to the fact that Wanda had insisted she and Darla (a ghost Wanda had made corporeal) needed to start fending for themselves. And 'fending for themselves' = getting jobs. While Darla was still trying to find her career path, I was only too happy to hire Libby—I needed all the help I could get.

Because Libby didn't believe women should compete with men in their work lives, she had no interest in becoming a realtor. Instead, she insisted her place be behind a desk as my secretary. And that was fine with me because I didn't have anyone to manage the phones or take care of other office responsibilities.

Libby was always very polite to the clients, but hopelessly judgmental. She never insulted or criticized anyone directly, but you *just knew* she disapproved of them, all the same. Despite her somewhat antiquated way of thinking, she was sort of like the mother hen of the office, checking in on each and every one of us, probably because she didn't have a husband to care for at home. Instead, she had her roommate, Darla.

As I arrived at the office, Bea was humming around the indoor plants, making them bloom so they added an outdoor feel to the place. We'd never had office plants during Ophelia's reign, owing to the fact that every plant she came into contact with withered and died within moments. Even if Ophelia *had* liked plants, they definitely didn't like her.

But back to Bea… she was one of my best employees—not only in her attitude, but also her work ethic. She was always so positive and no matter the situation, she seemed to improve it somehow. The flowers she'd coaxed into putting forth their best faces now made the office smell and look divine. And the little faerie seemed so happy with her efforts, she was actually exuding bright yellow light.

I walked by her and noted that her shawl had slipped off her shoulders, leaving her wings visible. They flashed up and down a few times, causing a ray of glittering, ethereal particles to sail through the air. The particles reflected the overhead lights, looking like tiny diamonds. Bea's wings changed color, depending on how the light hit them. Right now, they appeared to be sky blue on top and deep purple on the bottom—the same deep violet as her eyes which, yes, changed color depending on her mood, as well. It was one of the side effects of descending from the Spring Court.

She caught me looking at her wings and she blushed, pulling her velvet shawl back over her shoulders. The pink shade of her embarrassment spread across her face and dimmed the shine of her yellow glow. It was an odd effect, giving her the appearance of a neon sign that was backlit in a different color.

"Sorry, hon," she said, smiling sheepishly up at me.

"Don't worry about it, Bea," I said as I gave her a big smile. "No one in the office cares. Just hide them if a mundane drops in, okay?"

'Mundane' was the supernatural word for a human, someone without magic.

"Of course," she replied as she sauntered toward a stubborn Fichus tree that refused to keep his leaves intact. "Now you stop feeling sorry for yourself," she said, speaking to the forlorn tree in her happy sing-song voice, as if it could hear and understand her. For all I knew, maybe it could. It did look much healthier than it had a few days ago, at any rate.

Entering my office at the end of the hall, I dropped my bag into the chair beside the door and then watched as a frail looking little man passed by the window outside and then paused before entering the building. I could tell he was a mundane even from this distance. And though we did occasionally sell properties to mundanes, it wasn't that often. More so, since I'd taken over ownership—when Ophelia was in charge, she had a strict policy of refusing to sell homes to humans. Ophelia had been waging a one-person war against the unmagical, trying to ensure that only monsters lived in Haven Hollow.

Now that I owned the place, things were different, but I was still careful to keep up appearances. People without magic couldn't know about the supernaturals who lived among them—though there were exceptions —like Marty Zach, for example, but he'd signed a contract to ensure his silence.

While I'd made it my business to sell properties to humans and supernatural creatures alike, I was working on expanding my offerings to include less... *traditional* properties. There were those types of supernaturals who could live in typical houses, but there were other types of monsters who couldn't. I called those types of monsters 'exotics'. For example, most vampires required some type of cellar or below ground area to ensure they were entirely free from the sun. Dryads required homes surrounded by woods and werewolves were particular about doggy doors. Cellars, forests and doggy doors weren't such a tall order, though. What *was* a tall order was a house with ceilings high enough for a family of giants. Or a house without floors or concrete foundations so the forest Blights (sentient plant-like beings) could take root in the earth. Or a house with walls strong enough to remain intact during an ogre's moon rage (ogre PMS was something for the books!) Or a house maintaining a consistent temperature of below freezing, for an ice dragon.

I wanted to be able to appropriate homes for all types of monsters, exotics or otherwise. I wanted to get into the business of specialized homes, which, in some cases, could get downright weird. In fact, I'd been doing my best to court an exotic client with these exact needs. As such, I was nervous all morning and would have likely hyperventilated well before my morning coffee if not for Bea's positive vibes that did much to keep me calm.

I'd be having a conversation with my first exotic supernatural client later today—a grim named Darragh. Grims are spectral, dog-like creatures that haunt churchyards and protect the dead. I was scheduled to talk with Darragh in order to formalize plans to take him on a tour of a potential property tomorrow evening. He was looking for a new graveyard to protect.

There were two graveyards to choose from in Haven Hollow. The smaller of the two was situated between Poppy and Wanda's house and was called 'Hollow Cemetery'. The other was located on the opposite side of town and though it didn't have a name, the locals fittingly referred to it as 'No name Cemetery'. Neither was a church graveyard, as Darragh preferred, but he was willing to make do if it meant being able to live in a Hollow. Hollows were unique because they offered their supernatural citizens protection, thus Haven Hollow was in much demand among the paranormally inclined.

Regarding the cemetery between Poppy and Wanda's, it was a perfect plot for a grim. As nervous as I was about speaking to Darragh on the phone (because I'd never met a grim before, but understood they could be quite... moody), I was even more nervous about seeing him in person. Grims were known to be very proud and intensely serious. I'd heard they could be quite ferocious, too, if their territory was threatened. Just thinking about the particulars made me nervous. Lost in my thoughts, I jumped like a child encountering a real ghoul on Halloween night when the phone rang beside me.

I glanced at the clock and took a deep breath, steeling my nerves as best I could before answering.

"Hello! This is Fifi with Hallowed Homes," I said while smiling as widely as I could, a trick Bea had taught me. She believed she always sounded friendlier over the phone if she were smiling.

So that's exactly what I did.

Chapter Four

Darragh wasn't my first 'exotic' call of the week. In fact, I'd fielded several calls from other non-humanoid beings since I'd started reaching out to clients of their ilk. Most were still hesitant to get in touch with me on their own, though. Monsters, in general, were a distrustful and dreary lot, and the exotics were even more so. Usually, they sent the fae to contact me as their proxies. While it wasn't an unusual practice, dealing with middlemen definitely slowed the process. I supposed it wasn't that different from brokering a real estate deal in the normal world, outside Haven Hollow.

The fae were happy enough to become delegates, speaking on behalf of exotic supernaturals, in exchange for tithes, the details of which varied greatly from one species to another. Tithes were like I-O-Us—favors the fae could call in at some later time, when they most needed them.

Regardless, such was how Darragh had initiated contact with me—through a third-party elf called Cranough, but now Darragh was ready to speak to me directly. I almost wished we could go back to the third-party method because I felt much more confident when speaking to Cranough—he was much less intimidating.

"This is Darragh. I am calling to confirm our appointment details," a deep voice with a heavy Irish brogue announced from the other end of the line.

"Hello, Darragh, nice to hear from you," I responded, trying to sound like the confident woman I wanted him to believe I was, rather than the nervous bundle of nerves I actually was.

Upon my first introduction to Darragh, I hadn't spoken one word to him; Cranough had done all the talking for him. Now, it was something of a shock to hear Darragh's voice. My first meeting with Cranough had been brief, with the elf laying out exactly what Darragh was after. In response, I'd shown him both graveyards and Cranough had taken my recommendation of the cemetery between Poppy and Wanda's back to his boss.

Now, hearing Darragh speak for the first time, there was something about his voice that was completely unnerving. It reminded me of Lorcan's voice somehow, the only vampire in Haven Hollow. Lorcan's voice had the same deep timbre, but Darragh's sounded like it was almost more than one voice—like it had been multiplied from some deep, dark place, giving it a sinister, echoing effect. Plus, Lorcan's Irish accent wasn't as pronounced as Darragh's unless Lorcan was overly excited, upset, or drunk—which he often had been before Wanda came onto the scene.

It was Darragh's similarity to Lorcan that helped me to see him as less of a threat than he likely was. Lorcan and I were friendly with one another—he'd served as my landlord when I'd rented the opposite side of Wanda's duplex. After a disaster involving animate mold, I'd moved into another property of Lorcan's—this one much closer to the realty office.

I'd even allowed Lorcan to feed on me a few times. While that might sound scary or intimate, it really wasn't either. Being fed on by a vampire didn't have the same ramifications for someone like me as it did a mundane. There was no danger of Lorcan turning me into one of his own kind, and there was nothing sexual about it. Sure, the man had a reputation as an incorrigible flirt, but he was also one of the few men who didn't objectify me. And I'd always appreciated that about him. The only other men I could put in the same category were my old boss, Roy, who had become a good friend, and Marty Zach, whom I hoped would be more.

I was so used to men falling all over themselves around me, attracted by my succubus magic, that it was something of a relief when a man didn't—when he treated me like I was the same as any other woman.

I drove Lorcan from my thoughts as I tried to focus on what Darragh was saying. If I didn't know what he was (essentially a magic dog), his accent and deep voice would have struck me as kind of sexy. I could only imagine meeting him for the first time would almost be like meeting a blind date and then finding out your expectations exceeded the real person standing in front of you. No, a grim wasn't exactly an attractive option as a potential mate.

Did they even mate? I wondered, further unsure how they procreated… then I realized I might not want to know.

"This plot of land had best live up to your promises or I'll be more than a little put out," Darragh continued. "My time is valuable and I do not appreciate it wasted."

"I understand, and I'm sure the plot and the tomb

will stand up to your scrutiny. This is a very special piece of Haven Hollow history. And… as I told your proxy, Cranough, this particular location has many of the features you're looking for. The graveyard was the first founded in Haven Hollow and it's over one hundred years old, which should provide you with numerous spirits and graves to protect. The tomb, itself, belonged to none other than the founder of Haven Hollow, Jeremy Grenton Haven."

"Yes, the infamous gargoyle."

"Right."

"And the size of the tomb?"

"Is large… roughly fifteen feet by fifteen feet, and dates back to 1845. It's in the gothic style."

"And it's a freestanding tomb?"

"It is. It also includes Jeremy Genton Haven's sarcophagus in an arched recess that's raised on brackets. The tomb includes classical-style arches and columns and features sculptural portraits of the Haven family and a freestanding figure of the deceased."

"Is there more you can tell me about the plot?"

"Haven Cemetery also comes with a mausoleum containing several vaults, and I've already sold some of the vaults to our supernatural residents so you'll have them to guard in the coming decades. Until then, you'll be able to guard the mortal residents buried in the main portion of the graveyard and use your magic to shield them from any dark magic."

"Dark Magic?" Darragh repeated, sounding more interested. "And from where does this so-called 'dark magic' emanate?"

"Oh, from the Blood Witch who lives nearby." My mind shifted back to Wanda for a moment. She was actually excited about the prospect of having a grim around, because she was hopeful Darragh's power would keep her from inadvertently raising any zombies she didn't mean to reanimate.

"There is a Blood Witch in Haven Hollow?"

"Yes. I told your proxy as much."

"Has she claimed Sanctum?"

"Yes, and she's also on the council."

"I see," Darragh answered and paused for a few moments. "Then she still has her wits?"

I cleared my throat, finding this subject uncomfortable, because it was so personal to Wanda and yet... Darragh did have a right to know what was going on with Wanda if he was planning on taking residence in the cemetery. "She does."

"And the vampire who sired her?"

"He's her... friend."

"Then he hasn't lost his sanity either?"

"No, not that I'm aware of."

"Hmm... interesting." He paused for another few seconds. "Is this Blood Witch friend or foe?"

"Friend, most definitely."

"Until she turns."

I didn't know exactly what he meant, so I didn't respond.

"I am to understand this property possesses no church?"

"As I discussed with Cranough, there are no churches at either of our cemeteries in Haven Hollow, but I believe you'll be happy here even without a church on the grounds." And then I remembered the abandoned and somewhat derelict shack on a parcel of land just beside this one. "If you purchased the adjacent property to the graveyard, one with a shack of sorts already on it, you could build a church there?"

"Silly child," Darragh responded in a thundering voice. "*I* cannot build a church."

"Oh."

Darragh grew completely silent for a moment and I hurried to fill the silence, afraid I might be losing his interest. I really needed to make this sale because it was a big one. "There are also some marble statuaries on the plot, lots of ivy and full-grown Ash trees. As to the tomb, I could add furnishings and other details to provide for your comfort if you decide to make this purchase."

"I see."

"Once you've seen it for yourself, we can discuss any other measures that would be to your liking and maybe I can accommodate those too."

I didn't want to make any promises I couldn't keep, but I did want Darragh to understand I was willing to work with him and this sale was important to me. It was necessary for me to earn a reputation as someone who went above and beyond for her clients—that was the only way I could hope to draw the attention of the more exotic supernaturals.

At the same time, it was best not to show my hand entirely, even if I was willing to go pretty far to upgrade the property to suit Darragh, regardless of whether those upgrades meant me losing a bit of profit on the sale. If I could get someone as picky as a grim to buy one of my properties in the Hollow, that would only attract other, more specific buyers.

"Harrumph!" He sighed, exasperated. "I'll judge for myself upon seeing it. I'll be arriving tonight. Don't be late for our appointment tomorrow evening."

I started to say I wouldn't be late, but realized he'd already hung up. I looked at the receiver for a moment and then placed it back onto its cradle, figuring this conversation was the best I could hope for. Yes, Darragh was infinitely contrary and more than a bit frightening, but at least he seemed like he was open-minded about the place.

"How'd it go?" Bea asked from behind me, causing me to jump.

It was only then that I realized she'd been hovering. She was, no doubt, prepared to give me a pep talk if I needed one. I smiled at her, but then shook my head.

"I don't know. Darragh was hard to read."

Bea nodded. "Grims are notoriously cranky and difficult to deal with."

"I think the conversation might have gone over well, but I can't be sure until after the tour and well, I probably won't know his exact intentions until he actually purchases the place."

Bea nodded again. "If you want to do business with exotics, you'll have to get used to that. They aren't the easiest lot to deal with and some of them are downright impossible."

"Well, hopefully we'll start making a name for ourselves and Hallowed Homes will be the one-stop-shop for exotics."

"We are well on our way," Bea answered with a big grin.

I nodded. "This is a big positive for us—and the fact that Darragh is even coming out to see the graveyard is a pretty big deal."

"Just don't be put off by his appearance... and I guess you already survived his voice."

I looked up at her then, nodding in quick succession. "His voice was... *bizarre*. Almost like there were multiple people talking at the same time."

"It's the most terrifying thing about a grim—unless, of course, you cross their boundaries. Then, you're looking at an entirely different creature altogether."

"Have you known many of them?"

She cocked her head to the side as she pondered my question. "A few. I still hold tithes from a couple of them, actually."

"You used to act as a proxy?" I was surprised.

She nodded. "It's good to earn favors from powerful creatures." Then she sighed. "Someday, I'll call those favors in... when I need them most."

Then something occurred to me. "I hope Darragh doesn't think he's paying me in tithes."

Bea shook her head. "You would've had to sign a contract for him to think that and you kind of, sort of need to be fae in order to act as proxy. I mean... I've never heard of any other creatures doing it."

"Ah."

Bea nodded and continued with her explanation. "Cash is king and all that, but when you're in a real pickle, tithes aren't the worst thing to have on your books. Cash won't do you any good in a serious crunch with the wrong sorts. And tithes can be a far better bargaining tool than paper money sometimes."

"I'll keep that in mind if I'm ever offered any tithes."

"Chances are, you won't. Tithes are pretty much reserved for the fae." Then her expression dropped as she turned around and faced the front of the office. "Crap!" She said, disappearing from my doorway and hurrying down the hallway to employ her glamour in order to look 'presentable', as she called it.

I poked my head into the hallway in time to see a mundane walking through the door. I watched as Bea, having tucked her wings under her baby-blue cardigan, walked calmly back to her desk and sat down as Libby stood up to greet him.

I glanced back at the phone. A shiver ran through me just thinking about that echoing voice on the other end. I couldn't help but wonder if inviting in creatures like grims was a smart move, after all. Ophelia was a horrible boss, but she'd had a keen eye for business. And she hadn't gone after the business of the exotics. I had to wonder if there was a reason why.

The thought of Ophelia made my skin crawl, and I wondered at Bea's warning about seeing a grim in person. Would Darragh be more hideous than Ophelia had been? A night hag was a sight you didn't soon forget. I wasn't sure if I was up to having to face something potentially more hideous, much less do business with it.

Crap. I thought as I realized what I'd set myself up for... *Meeting a grim in an almost pitch-black cemetery, by myself...*

Don't forget you're a demon, Fifi, I reminded myself. *And a demon shouldn't be afraid of a dog...*

Chapter Five

Eager for a distraction after my conversation with Darragh, I hummed around the office, rearranging things I wasn't quite happy with. I moved some brochures to the front entrance and then paused as I turned around and tried to figure out what else I could busy myself with so I wouldn't have to focus on my nerves, which were getting the better of me.

"You need to get going," Libby called out to me. "You have a Council meeting in ten minutes."

"Thanks," I replied in my most positive sounding voice, but I really didn't feel like going. In fact, I was feeling bad altogether. I took a deep breath. "Is it hot in here, Libby?"

"Nope. Feels fine to me," she chirped, quickly returning to her desk to answer a ringing line.

I adjusted my collar, which suddenly felt way too constricting. The office was not only hot, but it was humid too—like a Louisiana swamp. I could feel sweat breaking out along my forehead and the small of my back, and I suddenly needed some fresh air.

Figuring I could kill two birds with one stone, I

planned to stop by the cemetery and clean up the tomb (again) before Darragh arrived to look at it. Even though I'd already tidied the place a few days ago, before Darragh's proxy had visited, I figured I could tidy it up again. After all, I needed it to be in premium order. Selling this graveyard to the grim would really get Hallowed Homes off on the right foot.

Plus, I didn't want to go to the council meeting, even if I had to be there. I'd just recently been voted onto the panel—as soon as I'd opened Hallowed Homes. In order to have a council seat, one had to own a business in Haven Hollow. Now that I did, Roy had nominated me for panel membership and the others on board had immediately agreed. So, I'd sort of been declared a member without having ever necessarily wanted to be one. But, I figured it would be good for business if I had a say in the way of things in Haven Hollow.

The council held bi-monthly meetings in order to keep a check on supernatural residents and the mundanes in Haven Hollow. The whole point of the council was to make sure we were doing our best to minimize supernatural exposure. If I didn't go to the meeting, no doubt, my brother Angelo, would try to step in for me and nothing good would come of that. Angelo had been more than irritated when I'd been given a place on the council and had already provided me with a list of issues he had with the way the council was running things. Not that I brought up any of those concerns because they were ridiculous in my estimation (the first item on his list was a complete segregation of mundanes and supernaturals).

Even though I was allowing Angelo to stay with me while his floors were installed, he was still annoyed with me because I'd refused to allow him to feed on his clients. His argument was that since Ophelia allowed him to do that and more, so should I. Honestly, he was just exhausting to deal with, but from where I stood, I didn't believe I had another choice. Angelo was my brother and if demons were anything, they were close-knit... or they were *supposed* to be. If I'd had my way, I would have sent Angelo back home to annoy our parents instead of me, but I guess you don't always get what you want. Besides, there was a tiny part of me that hoped maybe things between Angelo and me were improving slightly. There had been a few times when we'd gotten along decently well and my hope was that it would continue.

But, back to the council meeting—I had to go because I didn't want to chance Angelo trying to go in my absence. And even though I really wanted to double-check the tomb, there just wasn't time for it.

I grabbed my jacket and climbing into the 4Runner, headed over to the Half-Moon Bar and Grill, where the meeting would be held. Upon arriving, I noticed there were still some mundanes in the bar, but they wouldn't pose a problem, as we always reserved one of the back rooms intended for parties so we could have the privacy we required to conduct our meetings.

There was a time when I could hardly step into the Half-Moon comfortably. Men were wildly attracted to me for reasons they couldn't understand. Sure, I wasn't hard on the eyes. Great beauty was a part of my existence—it was part and parcel of being a succubus. My kind were meant to be beautiful in order to attract our prey, but that alone didn't explain the longing men felt in my presence. That longing wasn't owing to my beauty, it was owing to my pheromones. That's why I'd never felt comfortable taking advantage of mundane men, even though such was exactly what I was supposed to do in order to survive. I just hated the idea of robbing someone of his own free will.

Honestly, I hated having the kind of effect on men that I did. Luckily, thanks to Poppy and Wanda's powers, I could now walk into this place and others with relative ease.

As to the Half-Moon, I had to wonder if the air conditioning was out as I crossed the main dining room toward our meeting room. It was usually much cooler in here, but now it was very warm—unpleasantly warm even. Hmm, why was it so hot everywhere today?

I felt like I was in a sauna and very discreetly checked to make sure my armpits weren't visibly wet through my clothes. *Gross.* As far as I could tell, my anti-perspirant was doing its job. Sighing, I continued walking toward the room in the back, taking my seat on one side of the long table and greeting everyone as we all settled in.

As I sat there, waiting for the meeting to begin, my anxiety was at peak levels and the nauseous feeling I'd had earlier returned with gusto. In fact, I felt faint.

Why is it so hot and why do I feel so bad?

And then it dawned on me. I was low on energy, because I hadn't fed in far too long—the kiss I'd stolen from the man at the Black Bat hadn't been enough to soothe my starving body.

Maybe Bea is right and I should just have sex with a supernatural man and break this five year stint of abstinence, I thought to myself. *Then, at least, I wouldn't feel so crappy all the time.*

But, no, I couldn't wrap my brain around having a one-night stand. It just… it wasn't me. And it offended every romantic bone in my body. No, I'd just continue avoiding sex, like I had been, and I'd continue to rely on shallow feedings, taking a bit of energy from kisses here and there. Yet, I'd have to make sure those shallow feedings weren't so few and far between.

Yes, Roy had offered to appease me when I needed it and I'd shared a kiss with him, but somehow, the kiss just hadn't felt right—we were friends and until recently, he'd been my boss. Regardless, I hadn't taken him up on his offer and now I was suffering for that decision.

Soon, I was going to be forced to seek out a true mate—there was only so long my body could deal with this constant state of hunger. As to finding a mate, I wasn't sure how I was going to do so without using my supernatural powers of attraction, since I was hopeless at dating. And, I'm not exaggerating. Actually, 'hopeless' was probably too nice a word for my string of miserable relationships.

The more I thought about it, the more my thoughts returned to what Bea had said about just taking a lover for a night and never seeing him again. It would be the easy way out of this—the path of least resistance. As much as I hated that idea, I couldn't afford to get sick. I had a business to run, and I couldn't do that from a sick bed—and a sick bed was exactly where I was headed. If my body didn't get the life energy it so desperately needed, pretty soon I wouldn't be able to get out of bed at all.

I thought about my options—those men who were actual possibilities. Of course, Marty was at the top of my list, but getting involved with a mundane was a bad idea, no matter how much I might want to. There was no way Marty would be able to withstand my feeding from him. Besides, my experience in dating mundanes so far had been less than stellar. Then again, all my experiences had been pretty terrible. I was starting to believe I'd be forever single because nothing ever worked out between me and whatever man I was dating. What a sad excuse for a succubus I was.

Plus, I really liked Marty. He was the last person I wanted to use for a sexual thrill to feed my inner succubus. My interests in him were more than that. Lots more.

"Hey, Fifi. What can I get you?"

I looked up to see Shelby Stomper, a former co-worker, waiting to take my order. Roy had promoted her from a hostess to a waitress when I'd dedicated all my time to Hallowed Homes.

"Hey, Shelby. I'm actually not hungry but can I get a glass of ice water?"

"You've got it," she said and started to turn away, but apparently thought better of it and turned back to me. "You feeling okay, Fifi? You look a little pale."

Ugh, was it that obvious?

"Yeah. I feel fine. I just ate too many snacks at one of our open houses," I lied.

"Make a sale?"

"Not yet, but soon."

She nodded and offered me an understanding smile. "I'll get your water right away." She gave me a wink, moving down the table to get orders from the others as they piled in. Then she disappeared through the kitchen door with her order pad.

The meeting attendees were the usual suspects—Blood Witch Wanda Depraysie, vampire Lorcan Rowe, sasquatch Roy Osbourne, and werewolf Louisa Rutledge. The only one of us who was missing was centaur Stanley Stomper. It was then that Shelby returned with my water and a few other drinks.

"Stanley sends his regards, but he's at home with one of the girls who isn't feeling well," Shelby informed us.

"Good to know… let's get started then," Lorcan said as he took a seat at the head of the table. "I've got places to be and people to eat."

"Ha-ha, Lorcan, very funny," Wanda said with one trademarked arched eyebrow as she took the seat beside him. Wanda was very beautiful but in a macabre sort of way. An attractiveness kind of like Elvira's—good looking but offputting at the same time. Wanda was also one of those people you didn't want to cross because you wouldn't want to end up on her bad side. I was glad we were friends… or *friendly*. I didn't think Wanda really considered any of us to be her friends, except for maybe Poppy.

"Welcome, everyone," Roy said, choosing to ignore Lorcan—which was something he did often. The two didn't really get along very well. And that made sense because they were night and day different. Strangely enough, even though they were such opposites, I liked them both.

Roy sat down next to me and looking over, gave me a big and handsome smile. I returned it and then glanced around the table, noting that everything and everyone seemed a little fuzzy—blurry even.

"Because Stanley couldn't make it today, I'll be in and out to take his place," Shelby continued as she gave everyone a hurried smile and then disappeared again into the kitchen.

I sipped my water, not really feeling like drinking it, now that Shelby had brought it out. I was a little worried I might not be able to keep it down—I just felt nauseous suddenly—all part and parcel of this constant hunger that never fully went away. I tried to focus on something Louisa was saying about some mundane kids in the woods near her home that she'd had to scare away, but her voice sounded like it was being transmitted through the bottom of the mud bogs on the edge of town.

Taking deep breaths, I reminded myself the meeting wouldn't last too much longer and I could get through it, even as I wondered if I really could. Soon, everything began to disappear into the fog around me, growing grayer and less delineated. The gray fog began to move and swirl around me, making me even more nauseous as the spinning room enveloped me.

"Fifi, are you okay?" Roy whispered to me.

I looked up at him and nodded, though I wasn't sure I succeeded. "Does it seem dark in here?"

"Dark?" he repeated, frowning at me.

Suddenly, I felt like I was going to be sick, like I was going to throw up right in the middle of the table and ruin the meeting.

"Fifi?" Roy asked, leaning in closer to me as he put his hand on my bare arm. I could feel the energy coming from him and it helped to clear the fog in my head, but only a little.

All of a sudden, my body pitched sideways, as if I were getting sucked into the void around me. Roy lost his grip on my arm as I fell in the opposite direction, slipping through his fingers like a slippery eel through a large net.

I landed with a thud against the cold tiles of the event room, my heart slamming against my chest as everyone stared at me in shock.

Then everything went black.

Chapter Six

I awoke to find myself in a bed—not my bed, but someone else's. And that couldn't be good. Suddenly afraid I'd done something I'd soon regret, I sat bolt upright and looked around, all the while struggling to remember what had happened that would end with me being... *here*. I wasn't even sure where 'here' was.

The last thing I could remember, I was at the Half-Moon, trying my best to focus on the council meeting as if I were perfectly healthy and fine. Obviously, I wasn't. I breathed a sigh of relief as I glanced down and took in the fact that I was fully dressed. So, there was probably no possible way I'd had sex with whoever owned this house. And thank my lucky demons for that!

So how had I returned to consciousness, when I'd clearly been in such a bad way? I tried to take stock of my body and realized with growing horror that I felt... *better*, stronger, more energetic. Gone was that nauseous feeling and the incredible exhaustion. But, how was it possible that I felt better? I shuddered as the answer occurred to me: *I must have fed on someone.*

Yes, I had to have taken someone's life energy, otherwise I wouldn't have been able to come out of the state in which I'd been and, furthermore, I wouldn't feel even better now. But if I had fed on someone, who was it? Someone at the meeting? Hmm, feeding on one of them in my blackout and desperate condition could have done permanent damage.

Unless...

Unless I'd fed on Roy.

He was the only person in the meeting who could have withstood a full succubus feeding while the succubus in question was in a state of starvation. Sasquatches possessed superior strength and their life forces were almost indestructible. Roy was one of few species who could survive full, repeated feedings from a hungry succubus. Lorcan would have been strong enough to survive, true, but I wouldn't have gotten very far with him because he had no life force to give. He was powered by undead magic and that wouldn't help me.

No, it must have been Roy.

I took a deep breath as I worried just how far I'd gone with Roy (if he had, in fact, been the one to feed me, then bring me here). I didn't feel like I was filled to the brim with life force—no, I just felt marginally better than I had this morning. But I still had that ever-present feeling of malaise that had characterized me for the last five years, the last time I'd taken a lover. So, no, Roy and I hadn't had sex. And that was a big relief because sex would have just… muddled a friendship that had no business being muddled. Regardless, I still wanted to know exactly what we *had* done.

I struggled to my feet, and as strange as it sounded, I was grateful to find I was still a bit weak because that meant I hadn't broken my five year stint. Still, I didn't know where I was or how I'd gotten here, and that was causing me some stress. It was also the first order of business. I brushed my hands down, across my clothes, as I took a deep breath and hoped I was at Roy's. I glanced out the window and saw massive pine trees, but beyond them was the very tip of the white dome of Haven Hollow's church. That meant I was still in town —in the area that bordered the forest.

I had an inkling as to where I was now. Roy lived in Haven Hollow, but you wouldn't know it because his house was located in the thick forest near the town center, giving the illusion of a divide in dimensions.

As to the room around me, it looked pretty rustic with the roughhewn beams that formed the walls and the matching hardwood floors, the color of amber. The wood motif was continued in the planked ceiling— looking like an old cabin.

The decor could have been better—'sparse' was probably a good word for it. There wasn't any art on the walls, and aside from the worn plaid blue and red quilt on the bed, the room was lacking color. There wasn't even a rug on the floor—just a large dresser across the way and matching bedside tables on either side of me, one with a lamp.

As I continued to grasp my surroundings, the smell of woodsmoke assaulted my nostrils. Hmm, someone must have been tending the fireplace. With my heart in my throat, I padded into the hallway in my socks.

There wasn't much change between the bedroom and the hallway. Everything here was wood, too, and the hallway opened up into a decidedly 'wood' living room. It was then that I saw a man stoking the fire in a small, rock fireplace.

Roy.

I cocked my head to one side and admired his jawline which was captured by the flames behind him.

I'd never just looked at him before—studied him when he wasn't aware I was standing there, staring. But there was something comfortable about doing that now.

Roy was incredibly handsome, but I'd always thought so. Up until now, Roy's handsome face and big, burly body had always been one of those things I was aware of, but didn't give a lot of thought to: not much different from admiring a new dress or a field of freshly blooming flowers. But, now I noticed him and I enjoyed noticing him. Not that his being handsome changed my feelings for him, because it didn't. Roy was my friend, and that's exactly how I wanted things to stay. Given my history with relationships, this was one I wasn't willing to screw up.

Not only that, but Roy had dated Poppy for a while and even though their relationship was over, and he was now single, it went against girl code to even think of him as anything more than a friend… not that I *was* thinking of him as more because I was decidedly NOT. Besides, I was head over heels for Marty, despite how stupid that probably was.

I had a brief worrying thought as I wondered what Poppy would say if she knew I was alone with Roy and that I'd awoken in his bed. It just seemed so… intimate and Poppy was a good friend. So how would I explain this?

You just tell her the truth—that you blacked out and Roy came to your aid. She'll understand—besides, there's nothing going on between you and Roy anyway, so there's nothing to feel nervous or guilty about, I told myself. *In fact, you probably don't need to tell her anything at all.*

It was then that Roy looked up from the fire, spotting me in the doorway. For a moment, I was hit with a wave of passion that seemed to roll off him like a tidal wave. It hit me full force, and I took a step back as I tried to collect my wits and my breath. Then, as quickly as it had come, the strange sensation was gone, and in its place was an expression of surprise on his face.

Hmm, strange.

"Are you alright?" he asked as he swiveled all the way around to better face me.

"I… I'm feeling better."

He nodded and gave me a smile. "You gave us one hell of a fright."

"I'm sorry." I cleared my throat and then tried to remember just what I'd wanted to ask him. "Um… how long have I been out?"

"Maybe an hour?"

"Did I… did I feed from you?" I asked, though I already knew the answer. Of course I had.

"You came to a few times and… took what you needed from me."

"Oh," I answered, finding this conversation completely… uncomfortable. "Um… what does that mean, exactly?"

He looked at me and didn't seem to share my embarrassment. "It means you kissed me."

"Oh." I felt my heart drop to my feet before it started pounding, and I was sure I was every shade of red. "I'm… I'm sorry."

He shook his head. "Don't be. It wasn't like a kiss-kiss."

"A kiss-kiss?"

He chuckled, and the sound was deep and harmonious. "I mean… not on the lips. You could barely lift your head and it seemed enough just to give you my wrist."

"I kissed your wrist?"

He nodded, and I couldn't help the surprise that seeped through me. Usually I had to make out heavily with a man in order to get enough life energy from him. The fact that I was able to absorb Roy's power through simple skin-to-skin contact just hinted to his incredible strength.

The way he looked at me—his smile, his openness—revealed he didn't regret anything. And that was a realization that caused me some level of calm, even if I was still blushing like an idiot.

"Are you… are you feeling okay?" I asked, worried that maybe I'd taken too much of his life force, even as I realized such was impossible. As a sasquatch, his energy was basically limitless.

"I'm fine, Fifi," he answered and shifted his gaze back to the fire. I took a deep breath, only now realizing I'd been holding it. Exhaling, I then tried to understand the embers of lust that continued to burn deep in my belly. They just… made no sense to me. I shouldn't have felt this way about Roy—and I never had before, yet now…

I had to shake myself out of whatever insanity this was. Suddenly ashamed, I felt more heat claim my cheeks as I wondered what in the hell had gotten into me.

It's just the succubus hunger trying to take control of your body, I thought to myself and decided to go with that mode of thinking, because it was easiest.

I watched quietly as Roy stood up and approached me, towering over me, and nearly taking up the entirety of the small space in the living room. He was massive, yes, but standing before me now, he appeared even larger than I remembered. I swallowed hard as he walked across the room, never taking his eyes from mine. And his eyes suddenly reminded me of those of a predator—narrowed and focused. Intent. Truly, he was the ultimate of all predators—there was really nothing that could take a sasquatch down.

Even unleashing my full succubus on him, I wasn't sure which of us would win. Thank the demons it wasn't something I had to worry about.

For as much as I believed Roy and I would only ever be friends, I was firmly convinced he felt the same. Never in the time we'd worked together had he ever given me even the slightest hint that he was interested. Instead, he'd laughed at my ridiculous flings, given me advice, and treated me like the protective older brother I didn't have (Angelo wasn't much of a role model where older brothers were concerned).

Sure, Roy had kissed me once upon a time, but that kiss had just been a ploy—part of a larger plan to convince my family I wasn't trying to destroy the succubus side of myself (even though I had been). It was a ploy to make them believe I was feeding from men, and many of them. The kiss hadn't meant a thing, to either of us.

So, why was I staring at his lips now?

"I want you to talk to me, Fifi," he said and his deep voice reverberated around the small cabin, echoing off the walls and embracing me with its low timbre. And then there was his scent—a scent I was doing my best not to let go to my head. But it was ever-present—filling the air, seeping into the wooden walls and floors, rising up from the furniture. Roy smelled like the forest, like the earth and the rain, but it wasn't just a natural smell—he also smelled like everything masculine—spice, sweat and strength. He smelled like power.

Or, maybe that was just my succubus wanting to mate with him.

Mate with him! Fifi! I inwardly reprimanded myself. *Snap out of it or you're going to make a fool of yourself in front of Roy!*

I couldn't argue with the facts, though—and mating with Roy was exactly what the succubus wanted. Were I to leave things up to her, I'd have attacked him already, forcing him to the floor and taking whatever control he thought he had away from him.

Good thing the succubus wasn't in control.

"You… want to… to talk to me?" I asked. Why did I sound so breathless?

"Yes."

"About what?"

"About what's going on with you." He took the distance between us until only a few feet separated us. "I want to talk about what you're doing to yourself," he continued, his brow knotted together in some combination of concern and disapproval. "You're obviously still starving yourself and I'm not sure why."

"I don't know… what you're talking about." This was my business, and I wanted to keep it that way. Whatever I was or wasn't doing wasn't Roy's problem. But, how was I going to tell him that? Especially when he looked so determined to intrude, or 'help' as he termed it.

"I think you know exactly what I'm talking about."

"Why… why did you bring me here?" I asked, wanting desperately to change the subject.

He shrugged. "I figured you wouldn't want Angelo to find out you aren't feeding and haven't been."

I nodded, because he had a point. "Thank you."

"Talk to me, Fifi."

Chapter Seven

Talk to him…

I wasn't ready to face the subject of why I wasn't feeding. Instead, my brain was still wrapped around the fact that I'd fainted at the council meeting. "Everyone at the meeting saw me pass out?"

Roy nodded. "I made an excuse for you and said Bea mentioned you weren't feeling well. Then I said I'd take you home and… I brought you here instead."

"Thank you."

He narrowed his eyes. "Don't thank me. Instead, tell me what's going on."

"There's nothing going on, Roy…"

"Fifi."

"Really," I lied, giving him a false smile that I was more than sure he wasn't buying. "I'm not sure what you're worried about," I continued, feeling the sudden urge to flee. He was just so… intense… his gaze was so intense—the way he was shaking his head and folding his arms across his barrel chest was just so… *intense*. It was all I could do to keep my eyes level with his face, when all I wanted to do was hide. Well, the succubus wanted to do other things, but she didn't matter at this point.

"I know you know exactly what I'm talking about," he answered as his jaw grew tight and his eyes narrowed. "I thought we'd dealt with this whole subject already."

"Dealt with what subject?" I demanded, starting to get irritated because this was one topic I didn't want to discuss—it was just… personal and, more than that, it was embarrassing.

"Poppy created that repelling potion for you and I thought it had solved your problems, but it appears you're still denying yourself a basic need of your species."

"I don't want to talk about it," I answered snidely, folding my arms across my chest to match his own. Hopefully by giving him the same attitude he was currently giving me, we'd be at an impasse and he'd give up this interrogation.

"*I* want to talk about it, because I'm your friend and I care about you."

I couldn't meet his eyes. I was just suddenly flushing with embarrassment, with humiliation, anger and defensiveness. And his close proximity was doing all sorts of things to my inner succubus, things I didn't want to think about—things that made the shame rising within me do so on fast-forward. If Roy knew the thoughts and saw the images going on in my head… if he knew how much the succubus wanted him… I was mortified at the thought.

"What's going on, Fifi?"

"Nothing is going on," I spat back immediately, but he shook his head and reaching down, tilted my chin so I was forced to look up at him. His touch sent a shiver down my entire body and I could feel myself leaning into him, needing to absorb more of him, wanting to satiate myself with him.

"Don't lie to me."

"I… I don't… I don't know what you want me to say."

"I want you to tell me the truth."

My eyes narrowed as a feeling of indignation soared through me—who did he think he was, trying to force this out of me? Why couldn't he just deal with the fact that I didn't want to talk about it? Why was he making it such a big deal? "This isn't… your business, Roy."

He didn't back down. He just continued standing there, staring at me with an expression that was hard to read. "It is my business because I'm making it my business."

"Well, don't!" I yelled and his eyes widened in surprise at the same time mine did. This was the first time I'd ever raised my voice to him.

He paused a few moments, as if trying to get his thoughts in order, and then he took a step closer, reaching out and placing both his hands on my bare arms. His touch was warm and I could feel myself pulling his energy through his fingers, taking it into me. And his life essence felt and tasted incredible. His animal magnetism sunk into me, filling me with a wild energy I suddenly craved. I wanted more… *needed* more.

I stepped away from him, pulling out of his hold as I took a deep breath and felt light-headed. I had to get control of myself and I could only do that if I wasn't standing so close to him. I shook my head as I glanced down at the floor, unable to meet his gaze. "You can't… you can't touch me… for a little… bit, Roy."

"Why not?"

"Because," I said, taking another step back as I focused on his eyes again, instantly regretting it. Demons below, but he was more handsome than I'd ever realized! How was it possible I'd never felt this… urge, this need towards him before?

It has nothing to do with Roy and everything to do with the fact that he's a man, I answered myself.

"Because?" he repeated, reminding me I hadn't responded.

"I was pulling… your essence from you. I… I couldn't help it."

"I don't care."

I frowned, thrown off by his response. "But, it's not… right."

"You obviously need it."

He took the steps that separated us again and my heart started to pound in my chest, making me feel even dizzier. "I'm not… in full control of myself," I started, shaking my head as I tried to back away again.

He reached out and gripped my arms, not allowing me to further retreat. "I can take it, Fifi."

"No," I said, trying to break our connection. I was dangerously close to losing it completely, to throwing myself on him, and I desperately didn't want that to happen. He didn't understand what he was doing—he didn't understand how close I was to losing all control. "Please," I whispered.

He dropped his hands and took a step back as I breathed out my relief. I didn't want to, but I felt forced to look him in the eyes again. His were just so… raw… so full of feeling. It was almost too much to handle.

"I care about you, Fifi, and I don't want to see you hurting yourself."

"I'm okay," I whispered.

He shook his head. "You aren't okay. Look what happened today... you could have seriously hurt yourself, blacking out like you did. As soon as I saw you, I could tell there was something wrong... you looked sick."

"I'm not... sick. I'm fine."

"Then why aren't you feeding?"

"Because..." I took another deep breath, followed by another. The need, the desire to touch him was becoming nearly impossible to subdue. "Because... I don't want... to be what I am. I don't want... to be a succubus."

"You have no choice about that. It's what you are."

"I know but... that doesn't mean I have to like it." I could feel tears threatening my eyes. I took another few steps away from him, but he closed the distance immediately and I wanted to cry out at him to give me some space—to back up so I could catch my breath and will my heart to calm the hell down. He just... he was doing something to me—his proximity, his body, *him*.

"You are what you are."

I nodded and swallowed hard, wanting to turn around and run back into the bedroom where I could hopefully lock the door, with him on the other side.

"Well, I don't like it! I don't like anything about it." I forced myself to pay attention to the conversation, to channel the emotions within me into the words coming out of my mouth.

"Talk to me," he said.

"No," I started but lost the rest of the words. He just... he didn't understand that talking wasn't going to help me. The only thing that was going to help me would require the two of us with our clothes off.

Stop thinking like that, Fifi! I derided myself.

"Fifi," he insisted. It was obvious he wouldn't let up until I explained.

"I don't like the fact," I started, stalling to catch my breath. "...that I'm driven to steal the life force from others or... that I'm meant to use this power I've been given... to do nothing but bad things."

"You aren't a bad person, Fifi."

"Only because I'm constantly fighting my own nature!" I nearly yelled again. I was flushed and had to take a few seconds to let the air fill my lungs again. All the while, I was still fighting the demoness inside me who regarded Roy as a grade A steak.

"Then stop fighting it."

I shook my head emphatically. "I can't stop fighting it or I'll become... what I don't want to become."

"You could never be anything other than you, Fifi."

I shook my head, frustration starting to get the better of me. Roy just didn't get it! He didn't understand! He was talking about something he absolutely knew nothing about. "Look at Angelo! He's exactly what he's sup-posed to be, and he's awful!"

"You aren't your brother." Roy took a deep breath and reached for me again. He took my hand this time and my body instantly responded by absorbing his energy, allowing it to sing through me as my own strength started to increase. I felt my eyes flutter closed and the surprise over how easily it was to feed from Roy occurred to me again.

"Please, Roy..."

"The point is... you can't keep doing this to yourself," he continued, completely ignoring the fact that I was anything but comfortable. "You have to accept what you are. You have to make peace with it."

"I can't make peace with it because…" I opened my eyes. "Because I hate it!" I tried to drop his hand, but he wouldn't allow me. He held it tight and gave me a knowing expression. He understood I was pulling his life essence, but he didn't care. He was… offering himself.

"I don't think you're looking at the situation the right way," he answered, and I frowned because I wasn't sure what he meant.

"What other way is there to look at it?" I responded, my voice coming out winded—it wasn't easy to speak and to soak in his life essence at the same time. Furthermore, all I wanted to do was taste his lips again, feel his energy flowing into me and savor it. "I am what I am, just like you said."

He gripped my hand even harder and then pulled me into the breadth of his chest as I gave a shocked gasp and felt like I was about to lose all control right then and there. I had to close my eyes and remind myself to breathe in deeply and breathe out just as deeply. All the while, I was fully aware of the warmth of his skin, of the way he was now holding my hand and his other hand was wrapped around my arm.

"Look at me, Fifi."

I shook my head and kept my eyes shut tight. "I can't…"

"Open your eyes."

I shook my head again. "Roy, I'm… I can't control… I'm going to lose…"

"I don't care," he said and his voice took on a wild sort of growl I'd never heard before—it was as if his inner feral being was communicating with my own.

"You don't… know what you're saying."

When he spoke again, his voice was soft, and it tickled my ear. "If you were able to find a man strong enough to survive your feedings, you wouldn't have a problem with your nature."

"Right… but that's… impossible."

"Look at me." I forced my eyes open as he studied me and shook his head. "It isn't impossible. It just means you have a smaller pool of men to choose from."

I laughed, but the sound was acidic and when I tried to yank myself away from him, he fought me, holding me captive, forcing me to stand still. "A smaller pool than the already hopeless pool I've already been swimming in." I shook my head as the fire of desire within me started to turn into a fire of anger. "I've already come to terms with the fact that my love life is doomed. It always has been."

"So what's the alternative?" he demanded, almost angrily, though I wasn't sure why. "Just continue to deny your true nature until you lose it one day and do exactly what you're scared you're going to do? Drain someone to death?"

"Roy," I started, but he interrupted me.

"The Fifi I know wouldn't give up so easily. She is the most hopeful person I've ever met and when she sets her heart on something, she goes after it."

I didn't want to hear any of this. Deep down, of course I knew what he was saying was true, but I didn't want anything to do with it, all the same. Finding someone to date wasn't easy for me. I couldn't just go pick out some random guy on the street. I'd not fed properly for going on five years now and that meant my hunger was so immense that Roy was right, I'd likely kill whatever sorry man decided to get involved with me. A mundane wouldn't have a chance, which meant the object of my affection was definitely off limits. Marty could never withstand my hunger. At this point, I'd likely even hurt any of my monster peers by feeding from them.

All except Roy…

But, Roy was off limits because he and Bea were the closest friends I had. And there was his relationship with Poppy to take into account. Regardless, I had to do something. I might have another month, at best, until things got really dire. In the meantime, I had a business to run and no time for blacking out during council meetings or client showings.

Client showings…

Darragh! I was supposed to go to the graveyard and make sure it was ready for my meeting with Darragh and Cranough tomorrow evening! And, yes, while I definitely still had plenty of time to do so, Roy didn't need to know that. This was the perfect excuse to make my escape.

"I have to go." I tried again to break Roy's hold but he wouldn't release me. Even so, I refused to look at him and stared at the dancing flames of the fire instead. "I have… I have a meeting with an important client, Roy, and I don't have time…"

"Your client can wait. You're in no shape to leave yet, Fifi. You haven't fed enough—I can see it."

"He *can't* wait. This is an important—" Yes, I was lying about the timeliness aspect to my meeting with Darragh but this was the only excuse I had to get away from Roy, so I was going with it.

"Take what you need from me, Fifi," he interrupted, his voice soft again and his eyes searching mine.

"I… I can't," I answered and tried to pull away from him, but he held me so hard, I felt like I was in iron manacles. "I… have to go."

"You know as well as I do that you aren't satisfied.

You need more. So take it."

I inhaled deeply. "You don't understand, Roy… I *can't*."

He nodded. "You can."

"No."

"Take what I'm offering."

And that was when I lost the battle with the succubus.

Chapter Eight

I jumped up onto my toes, looped my hands around his neck, and pulled him down towards me as I snared his lips with my own. He made a surprised sort of sound, but as soon as my mouth touched his, he looped his arms around me and kissed me back.

I lost myself in our embrace, forgetting everything but how he felt and tasted. It had been a long time since I'd been so close to a man I couldn't harm, and now I allowed myself to just enjoy the feel of him, the taste of him. His energy was right there, on the tip of his tongue, mine for the taking. I let myself give in to that overwhelming urge, groaning as his taste flooded me.

His energy felt wild. It was peppered with the feral beast of the sasquatch—unruly, beyond powerful and wise. A shiver ran through me as I soaked in his power, not holding back this time. I felt him shudder as I sucked his strength out through our joined lips and tongues, the invisible streams of power flowing from his body into mine. Neither of us could see it, but we could both feel it, even beyond the kiss.

Everywhere our skin touched was a conduit between

us, pulling his life force into my hungry body. I took only what I needed, but still much more than what I would have taken from a human. What I'd already drained from Roy would put any mortal down for the count. Yet, it barely made a dent in Roy's energy store. Soon my dizziness and hunger pangs were things of the past and though I still wasn't one hundred percent, I was considerably better. As to Roy, I suspected it would take a couple of days of marathon sex for him to feel even slightly exhausted from the energy loss.

Marathon sex...

The brief thought that I could pull him towards his bedroom so I could drain what I wanted from him briefly flitted through my mind. I could break this five years of misery. I could allow the succubus to come to the forefront—doing so wouldn't hurt Roy. He was strong enough to withstand it.

It was then that he pulled away and when he did, I realized there was an expression of shock in his eyes. I felt my heart plummet as the reality of what I'd just done and what I was contemplating doing hit me like an anvil. I'd let this go too far—*way too far*.

I took a step back, the thought of seducing him bringing my mind back to full clarity and sending the hunger away for the time being. I took stock of myself and realized I was panting, flushed. I could blame the reactions all on my hunger, but I knew it was more than that. I wanted Roy—in that moment, I'd absolutely wanted him and even as I stood here, I *still* wanted him. And that realization bothered me... a lot. Yes, part of me felt as if I shouldn't have been surprised—Roy was larger than life, kind, funny and so handsome. But, I'd never thought of him as anything other than a friend, until this very moment, a moment I now wished sorely had never happened.

"I… I wasn't expecting that," he said with an apologetic smile.

"I'm sorry! I was trying to warn you," I started, feeling the sting of humiliation flooding me. "The succubus is getting more and more difficult to control. I didn't… I didn't mean to take advantage of our friendship and I..."

"No," he said, and held up a hand to silence me. "It's okay, Fifi, it just took me… by surprise, that's all. I figured you just needed to touch me to take my energy."

I nodded and suddenly felt like crying. More than that, I wanted to get out of his house pronto. I'd already made such a fool of myself.

And to think I was probably seconds away from trying to lure him into his bedroom. I was out of control! Not to mention, there was still the issue of my friendship with Poppy and my feelings for Marty—feelings I was already starting to second guess.

No, I told myself. *You do have feelings for Marty, and those feelings have nothing to do with the succubus within you. She was just determined to feed, and it didn't matter who from. And as to Poppy…*

"I don't mean…" Roy started, interrupting my thoughts as he then shook his head, rubbing the back of his neck like he did when he was frustrated about something. "I hope I didn't embarrass you?"

He looked at me then and I felt like I was going to melt into a puddle on the floor. This whole thing wasn't embarrassing—it was humiliating. "No," I started.

"It's just… you and I are friends and we always have been," he continued. "And I just got out of a relationship with Poppy and I'm…"

"It's okay, Roy."

"I'm not sure I'm completely over it yet, to be honest."

"Roy, you don't have to explain yourself." I took a deep breath, trying to give him a smile of comfort, of understanding, even if I found it insanely impossible. All I wanted to do was run away and hide, to lick my wounds alone. "It was my fault and I shouldn't have… done what I did."

"It's okay," he replied softly.

Then there was silence—long, uncomfortable and heavy silence. We both just stood there, looking at each other, as if hoping the other would break it.

"Fifi," Roy said at last. "I want you to know that… my pulling away… it had nothing to do with you."

"It's okay," I almost interrupted. The last thing I needed right now was the 'it's not you, it's me' talk.

"Of course, I find you beautiful—I mean, how could I not?" he continued as I withered even more on the inside. "I can't say I haven't had an idle thought here or there."

"Roy…"

"I just… I'm not ready to even think about anything with anyone after what happened with Poppy."

Poppy… Oh, demons below. How would I live with the guilt of what I'd just done—forcing myself on Roy, on Poppy's ex! And Poppy was my friend! She was the reason I was living a semi-normal life for the first time ever. And look how I'd repaid her! By throwing myself at her ex!

He inhaled and then exhaled. "I've been really focusing on myself and trying to make sense of everything that happened between Poppy and me."

I just stood there awkwardly, not knowing what to say in response. He took a deep breath, seeming to try to recenter himself, and then continued while I maintained my slack-jawed silence.

"I just want to clarify what I was offering," he continued.

"You really don't need to."

"I'm happy to provide whatever sustenance you need because I hate seeing you denying your own true nature. I just... I figured that sustenance could be given in a... *friendly* way."

"It can," I started, although I wasn't sure just how friendly it could really be. I mean, a succubus by nature was a sex demoness, so what was Roy thinking my feeding from him would really look like?

"And... like I said, I just got out of a relationship," he continued awkwardly. "You know all about that so I don't need to get into it." He took a deep breath and then looked out the window behind me, as if he were lost in a memory. "I have a lot of thoughts about what happened between Poppy and me, but I'm still not sure how to feel about any of it," he continued, more to himself than to me.

"Roy," I started, wanting to spare us both this total embarrassment. "It's okay. You don't need to say any-thing more—I get it."

"We're friends and as your friend, I'm simply offering you something you need. You can feed on me without worry but, can we do so as... friends?"

"Yes," I answered, even though I had no intention of ever feeding on him again. Everything that had just happened was just way too... humiliating. Regardless, I had a feeling this awful conversation was finally over and maybe I could make my escape sometime soon. "Anyway, I really need to get going."

"I understand," he answered and moved aside so I

could walk to the door. I didn't waste any time and practically ran for it, reaching for the doorknob as something occurred to me and I turned to face him.

"Um," I started as we both stood there, looking awkwardly at each other for a moment, until I finally gathered my wits enough to speak. "I don't know how Poppy would react to what… just happened, especially so soon after you've broken up… even knowing that this… is just a means to an end for me."

"I won't say anything to her."

I nodded. "I don't want to feel like I'm keeping something from her, but I also don't want to upset her. She's my friend…"

And, besides, this is never going to happen again, I told myself, *so it can be a thing of the past, the exact place where it's going to stay.*

He sighed, long and hard. "She's my friend too," he said and then shook his head and appeared like he had a lot on his mind. "Though I'm not sure how true that is. I still have feelings for her, and I don't know when or if they'll subside. And… there's a part of me that wonders if maybe the two of us… could still work things out."

"I hope you both can." There was nothing but truth in my statement, even if the succubus warred against it.

"I'm not so sure… maybe it's a stupid idea…" His voice trailed off and his gaze was drawn toward the fire as he said something that cut me to the quick.

"I'm pretty sure Marty is using our breakup as his chance to move in on her, anyway."

"What?" I asked, even as my stomach dropped down to my toes. "What do you mean?"

He shrugged. "Just that the few times I've run into her since the split, he's always with her."

My heart started to calm down. "They're just really

close friends, Roy."

He chuckled but the sound was sour. "Sure, because that's all she's allowed them to be. Everyone knows he's crazy about her and always has been."

The words landed like a pile of stones in the pit of my stomach. Sadness washed over me like a cold stream, causing a contradicting sensation of pain and numbness and envy to take turns attacking me.

"Oh," I said and didn't mean to sound so crestfallen, but there it was.

"Not that it's any of my business anymore," Roy continued, again more to himself than to me.

And suddenly, it was all too much—Marty and Poppy, Roy and me, Roy and Poppy... "Anyway, like I said, I've really got to get going," I said, suffocating on my need to escape. "Thanks for what you did for me today." I put on my shoes and gathered my things.

"Are you sure you feel well enough?"

"Yes, I feel great," I lied.

I didn't wait any longer, but hurried out the door before I found myself saying something else to make things even more awkward between us. When I stepped outside, I breathed a sigh of relief and took stock of my surroundings.

On this side of the woods, it looked like I was smack dab in the middle of a forest, but as soon as I exited the tree line, I'd find myself standing on the sidewalk, opposite the town square. The path leading through the trees was almost non-existent, but I was still able to make my way without getting snagged on too many bushes. On the other side of Roy's house were more trees. They surrounded the house so that it was completely hidden from the town in front and the river that flowed in back.

I moved through the woods toward town quickly, buzzing with Roy's energy flowing through me, even as I couldn't get memories of what had just passed between us out of my head. I couldn't believe I'd come onto him! I couldn't believe I'd been so callous about our friendship and so selfish. And then there was Poppy to think about—had I broken the girl code? I was sure I had.

It will never happen again! I promised myself. *You lost control of yourself momentarily and that was it. Roy is just your friend and he'll remain your friend. Poppy never needs to know and hopefully, they'll get back together and live happily ever after!*

Yet, the burn of his refusal stung like all hell. And no matter how mortifying my thoughts, I could still feel his mouth on mine. And I could still taste him. Neither memory was quite as bad as it should have been.

Chapter Nine

The next morning I found myself sitting in my office and though I tried to pay attention to the day ahead of me, my thoughts kept returning to the day before and the kiss I'd stolen from Roy. The kiss had left me full of energy, but completely deflated in the confidence department. If I disliked the succubus within me before, I hated her now.

"You've got a visitor!" Libby said as she poked her head into my office and nearly gave me an apoplexy.

"A visitor?" I repeated, once I was able to catch my breath.

I was barely able to get the words out before Marty Zach walked through my office door, nearly giving me another heart attack.

"Hope I'm not interrupting," he said, and I noticed his hands were behind his back and he was wearing a big, goofy grin, looking like a giant twelve-year-old boy even though he was in his forties.

"No... no... you're not interrupting." I stood up and walked into the center of the room to greet him as Libby closed the door behind us. My heart was pounding in my chest the whole time and I suddenly wished I'd worn something a little more daring than the black slacks and navy turtleneck. "What can I help you with?" I asked, surprised because we didn't have the sort of friendship where he'd just show up at my office randomly. "I don't suppose you're interested in buying or selling a house?"

He chuckled and shook his head, and his longish hair fell into his eyes. Usually his hair was short, but this look suited him as well. It seemed any look would suit him—he was just that handsome. He was also tall—not as tall as Roy and nowhere near as broad—but Marty was still well over six feet and, as such, I had to look up at him. And his little gut didn't bother me either—it almost added to his boyishness.

We both just stood there, about five feet from each other, as I wondered if I should have given him a hug to say hello. Marty and I didn't know each other well, but we were friendly enough. Thinking I should have given him a hug, I suddenly lunged forward at the same time he did, bringing his hands from around his back and shoving a wrapped present in front of me. My chest slammed into the gift at the same time he brought it forward and we both gasped.

"Oh, I'm sorry," I said as Marty said, "I brought you a present."

I immediately took a step back, feeling heat claiming my cheeks. "I was… trying to give you a hug to say hello," I explained, not wanting him to think I'd just tried to attack him or something.

"Oh," he answered and then stepped forward, wrapping one of his arms awkwardly around me as he held the other one with the gift straight out the opposite way. I patted him on the back like he was a trusted dog and then separated myself, taking a step back as I wished the floor would rip open and swallow me whole.

Marty cleared his throat. "I've been meaning to come by to bring you a housewarming," he started, then looked around my office before correcting himself, "a *business-warming* gift."

"You brought me a business-warming gift?" I asked, touched, even though I'd never heard of a business-warming gift. Furthermore, it was wrapped in bright red Christmas paper with little Santas on Harley motorcycles.

"Sure did," Marty answered and held the parcel out to me with both hands. He smiled again and his blue eyes sparkled with excitement.

All the while, I wondered how I could have thrown myself at Roy when my feelings for Marty were just as strong, if not stronger, than they always had been? Damn the succubus within me!

I accepted the gift, which was maybe two feet tall and one foot wide, and looked down at it before looking back up at him. "Should I open it now?"

"Yes, please!" He cleared his throat. "Sorry about the paper, but it was all I had."

"Oh, that's okay," I answered, and when I looked up at him, I found his big, blue eyes focused on the gift in my hands. Excited anticipation dripped off him as he looked from the gift to me and I found myself admiring the expression on his face. There was just something so innocent about him—something that seemed untainted by the trials and tribulations of adulthood. It made being around him feel... good. Really good. I took the package over to my desk and carefully slipped my index finger beneath the wrapping.

"I hope you like it," he said, almost sounding shy.

"I'm sure I will," I answered as I freed one side of

the paper and started on the other. "And I'm really touched you thought of me."

"What kind of friend would I be if I didn't?" he asked and the word 'friend' slightly rubbed me the wrong way. But, I decided to let go of the feeling because I wasn't sure whether or not 'friend' really described the way Marty felt towards me. I mean, it had to mean something that he'd brought me a gift, right? As far as I could tell, men in general weren't the most thoughtful—anyway, they were nowhere near as thoughtful as women were. And yet, here was Marty, with a gift he'd not only wrapped (albeit not very well—it looked like he'd used a whole roll of tape) but he'd also put some thought into picking it out for me. Yes, that had to mean something.

Hmm, maybe my thoughts about Marty only having friendly feelings towards me were completely wrong? It wouldn't have surprised me if such were the case because I was pretty dense when it came to reading men and their interest. Sure, I could tell when a man wanted to have sex with me (which was pretty much always the case when I wasn't using my repelling potion) but as far as a man wanting something more serious with me? It had happened so rarely, I wasn't really sure what it looked like.

Maybe… it looked like this?

I finally managed to remove all the wrapping paper and the tape. And I was rewarded with a brown, cardboard box.

"Open it!" Marty nearly sang from behind me.

I laughed and then grabbing some scissors nearby, slit the tape down the seam of the box and opened it up, noticing green and red tissue paper crammed within. Reaching inside the box, I felt something cold and gripping it with both hands, yanked it out of the tissue paper. And then I was a bit... perplexed.

"Do you like it?" Marty asked, his crooked smile broad and his expression expectant.

"Um, yes!" I said, though I was still trying to figure out what it was. As far as I could tell, it was a ceramic statue from the Wizard of Oz—the scene where Dorothy lands her house on the Wicked Witch of the East.

"Do you get it?" Marty continued as I looked over at him, still completely puzzled. I mean, I knew *what* it was, but I still wasn't sure what it had to do with me or why he'd given it to me.

"Get it?"

He nodded. "Yeah, you're just like Dorothy."

"I am?"

He nodded even more rapidly this time. "Dorothy killed the Wicked Witch with her house, right?"

"Right."

"And you and Wanda got rid of Ophelia and now you've got yourself a new business!"

"Oh," I answered as I looked back at the statue and wasn't sure what to think of it or the reasoning behind it. Yes, I understood the similarity (sort of, but it was also a bit of a stretch. It wasn't like Wanda and I had dropped a house on Ophelia) but no, I wasn't sure I liked the reminder.

I looked back up at Marty and found his expression faltering. "Thank you so much!" I said, beaming broadly because I didn't want to appear ungrateful and I really didn't want to hurt his feelings. Especially because he'd put so much thought into this very odd gift.

"Pops warned me that it might be a bit too weird," he admitted with a shrug and a sigh, his shoulders slumping a little. 'Pops' was his nickname for Poppy and

I was fairly sure he was the only one who called her that.

"No, it's not too weird," I said immediately, not wanting him to think I didn't appreciate it. Because I did. "In fact, I love it and I'm going to put it right here on my desk, where everyone can see it!" I said as I placed the statue down on my desk and then took the steps that separated us, looping my arms around his chest as I thanked him again.

This time, he hugged me properly, and we just stood there, holding each other for a few seconds too long. And that had to mean something too—I mean, *neither* of us pulled away. He finally separated himself, clearing his throat, and then gave me another boyish smile.

"I'm really glad you like it."

"I love it!" I answered, which wasn't exactly the truth, but I appreciated the gesture all the same. And the fact that Marty had thought about me—it was enough to make my whole day.

"I'm so glad to hear that!" he said and beamed. "But, wait… there's more."

"More?" I asked a little hesitantly, wondering if he was about to produce more strange statues that were in somewhat bad taste.

He nodded. "I also wanted to let you know I'd happily exorcise any ghosts that might be hanging around this place and I'll do it for half-off—just a hundred bucks–it's my friends and family rate."

"Oh," I started, frowning as I wondered if maybe I would have liked a statue of the cowardly lion or the tin man better. "I don't think Hallowed Homes is haunted."

"Well, just in case you find it is, or a ghost decides to move in or something, the offer is always there."

I nodded as he nodded and then we both just stood there, not saying anything but just nodding like two awkward high-school kids at their first dance.

"I appreciate it, Marty," I said finally as he gave me another winning smile and then turned towards the door as if he were headed out.

"Well, I better get going because Lorcan's in the back of the hearse and he doesn't like it when I stay in one place too long."

I frowned and watched as he paused at the threshold of the door, turning around to face me again. "Isn't Lorcan asleep?"

Marty nodded. "Yeah, but I think he's got video cameras wired in the hearse somehow because he always seems to know what's going on, even when he's supposed to be asleep in his coffin, dead to the world."

I couldn't help but laugh, yet at the prospect of Marty walking out my door, I suddenly jumped forward and gripped his hand, not even realizing what I was doing. He glanced down at our joined fingers before looking back at me in surprise. I was just as surprised.

"Oh, um," I started and then patted his hand as my cheeks flushed red with embarrassment. What was wrong with me? "Could I, um… take you out… for dinner one of these nights?" I nearly choked on the words as I realized what I was doing. I was asking him out? *Me?* I was asking a man out? Demons below, but I'd never done anything like this before and the anxiety within me was at an all-time high. "I mean… to properly thank you for the gift?"

"You don't have to thank me for the gift, silly."

"I know but," I started before he interrupted me.

"Yeah, sure, let's grab dinner. You wanna tell Roy and I'll let Pops know?"

I felt a stab of disappointment but then figured he just didn't understand that I was asking him out… on a date… and not as a friend. I figured this was one instance where I'd have to be a bit… clearer. Marty could be a little bit… dense sometimes. I took a deep breath and couldn't hold his gaze—this was just… too embarrassing. "Oh, well… I sort of meant… I mean, I kind of was thinking maybe the two of us could just go?"

"Alone?"

"Well, only if you want to," I added, feeling my heart pounding against my chest as my breathing hitched, and this time I wished Dorothy would drop her house on me.

"Oh, sure," he said hesitantly as he considered it. "We could do that."

"Do you want to just text me?" I asked, wishing I hadn't put my foot in my mouth by asking him out because he clearly appeared… taken aback. Maybe I'd misread his interest? Maybe he did just want to be my friend?

"Sure, I'll do that," he said and then bee-lined for my office door. He turned around once he reached it, gave me a big smile and waved, then disappeared into the hallway as I sunk into my desk chair and wondered if this day could get any worse.

Chapter Ten

My meeting with Darragh came all too quickly. My nerves were still in a bunch as I arrived at the graveyard and watched the sun disappear over the numerous tombstones. As was customary with supernatural creatures, I was meeting Darragh at night—when he was active.

I'd arrived a little early and now willed myself to remain the picture of professionalism as I faced the entrance to Hollow Cemetery. I could see Poppy's house in the distance and as soon as I did, a feeling of guilt welled up within me.

Whatever happened between you and Roy is a thing of the past and it will never happen again, so you don't have to feel bad about Poppy, I reminded myself. *You didn't mean anything by it and feeding from him was simply a means to an end. And that was all it was. Besides, you need to focus on this sale!*

And I was right. I needed to project confidence if I was going to interest Darragh in purchasing this plot. Not to mention, I needed this sale desperately. I had to show my employees, especially my brother, that Hallowed Homes would succeed. Not only succeed, but that it would thrive under my new sales model.

As much as I was anxious about not being able to pull this sale off successfully, I was equally as nervous about the possibility of running into Poppy, either during or after the tour of the tomb since her house was so close.

And if that did happen, how would I ever keep my guilt to myself, especially coming face-to-face with her? I was a terrible liar, and that meant I wouldn't be able to keep myself from telling her what had happened with Roy.

And what then? I asked myself. *What if she thinks you broke girl code and hates you forever? What if she thinks you're a horrible friend?*

It was a thought I couldn't even stomach because I cared about Poppy and I cared about her friendship. And at the realization that I could have threatened that friendship, that I could have possibly broken it by kissing her ex-boyfriend… the shame was almost enough to do me in right there.

Then, there was the matter of Marty. Could it have been true what Roy had said—that Marty was crazy about Poppy? I mean, on the surface, of course it could be true, because really, why *wouldn't* he be crazy about her? They were already good friends, and she was as adorable as adorable could be, so why wouldn't he have the hots for her?

But, if he did have the hots for her, did she know about it? And did she feel the same? The thought made me sick to my stomach. I'd just… I'd had a crush on Marty for quite a while now, and the possibility that nothing would ever happen between us was almost too much to face. And yet, when he'd come to my office to give me that strange gift, he'd seemed... interested, hadn't he? Or had he? Hmm, I wasn't really sure. Marty was a hard one to read.

What's the point of wishing there was something between the two of you, anyway? I asked myself. *You're a demon and he's a human.*

Of course, I was aware that I could kill Marty with my succubus powers if I ever fed from him, but that was only if I was careless. I'd dated human men before and I'd managed not to do any of them harm... so there was always the possibility that I could figure things out with Marty.

My mind drifted back to the kiss I'd shared with Roy. It had been rattling around in my brain since it happened and no matter how many times I tried to force it back into the closet with all my other shameful memories, it wouldn't go willingly. I was sure it was just the succubus acting up, wanting more of him.

It had been a long time since anyone had satisfied my hunger, a long time since I'd let anyone satisfy it and no one had ever come so close with nothing more than a kiss. I couldn't help but wonder what it would be like to have Roy as my lover. I suspected I'd hardly need to feed from him at all, at least not on a constant basis.

Furthermore, if Roy were my lover, I'd probably feel almost human most of the time—a thought I could barely wrap my brain around because it just seemed so impossible. For the last five years, I hadn't felt like myself. Sure, I'd put up appearances, pretended to be happy, when the truth was that I knew my body was suffering—that *I* was suffering. But, really, how could I not suffer when I required sex in order to function properly? And now, at the thought that feeling vibrant and healthy was just a lover away, I felt a strange sense of hope swell within me.

But, just as quickly as the thoughts bounced into my head, I forced them out again. It did no good to think about things that couldn't be. Lusting after Roy was stupid, because he clearly wasn't over Poppy, he wasn't interested in me and I wasn't interested in him! Furthermore, I didn't want to do anything to jeopardize my friendship with Poppy or with him.

If you haven't already jeopardized both friendships by forcing yourself on him.

I took a deep breath and refocused my thoughts as I stepped out of the 4Runner and did my best to focus on this meeting, and not on the expression of shock that had been in Roy's eyes after I'd kissed him. Demons below, I'd made a fool of myself!

As I walked through the wrought iron gates that stood at the mouth of the graveyard, under the sign which proclaimed it to be: Hollow Cemetery, I immediately noted it was oddly quiet tonight. There were no animals stirring and the hum of insects was strangely absent. Even the wind, itself, which had ruffled the hemline of my blouse when I'd stepped out of the SUV, was now nowhere to be found. Instead, the air was stagnant. And even with the moon proudly glowing from the night sky, it still seemed unnaturally dark.

There was also an odd scent in the air and the scent stopped me dead in my tracks. I turned around, inhaling deeply as I took in all the tombstones that lay scattered around me. The smell hung heavy and hinted at something vaguely rotten. When I turned around and faced forward again, the scent seemed to dissipate. I took a few steps along the rocky path that wove between the graves, and the scent hit me full-force again. And yet, I couldn't determine where it was coming from.

The darkness and the rotting air made the cemetery even creepier than it otherwise appeared and I hoped Darragh wouldn't keep me waiting long. As far as I could tell, I was the only one here. There hadn't been any vehicles in the parking lot and as I turned around to face my surroundings now, all that greeted me were the outlines of the tombstones. I wasn't one to spook easily, but I had goosebumps. I glanced up at the moon to find it hidden behind the clouds, giving the whole place an even more sinister and gloomy feel.

I wanted to laugh at myself because how could someone who chose to do business with monsters be so skittish? It was ridiculous. Not only that, but I was a demoness—I should have felt at home with the dark and the things that lived in it. Angelo wouldn't have been afraid, that much was certain. Still, a shiver ran down my spine as I made my way through the graveyard toward the tomb in question, still feeling more than a bit out of sorts.

It's just nerves, I told myself.

I heard a sound off to my right and with my heart in my throat, immediately turned in that direction, but there was nothing there.

"Darragh? Are you here?"

When there was no response, I faced forward again, keeping my eyes glued to the shape of the tomb that was maybe twenty feet from me. Everything was still so eerily quiet—the whole scene was unsettling. At least that awful odor was now completely gone.

I walked toward the tomb, and noticed with a sense of forlorn dismay that the door was already open. I had to wonder if Darragh and Cranough had arrived early and viewed the tomb without me. For all I knew, maybe they were still inside it. I stuck my head in, but didn't see anyone. In fact, it didn't look like the space had been disturbed since I was last here, other than the door being open.

So, where was the grim and his elf proxy?

Maybe they're just running late...

Hoping such was the case, I stepped away from the door and then walked toward the back of the tomb to get a better look across the rest of the cemetery. My eyes were beginning to adjust to the darkness when the moon finally decided to slip out from behind the clouds and cast milky rays of light around the place, throwing strange shadows as it did so. Regardless, I could finally see more than an inch or two in front of me.

As I walked around the back of the crypt, I called out again to let Darragh know I was there, in case he hadn't heard me before, but there was still no answer. And the burgeoning sense of concern I'd felt earlier started to grow until it became an all-out worry. A few more steps and I stopped in my tracks, unable to go any further.

My heart rode up into my throat and my breathing stopped as I stood there, transfixed—both shocked and in denial at what I was seeing—unable to process the scene before me.

It was a body.

And not just any body.

"Oh, no," I finally gasped, feeling the air returning to my lungs as I took a deep breath and felt like I was going to pass out. Part of me wanted to run, but the other part wanted to find out just who this body was.

It was sprawled face down in the dirt, arms extended out to its sides. The hair was mussed, but long and dark orange. On autopilot, I bent down and touched it, hoping whoever this was might still be warm—that there might still be life left in there somewhere. But, the corpse was as cold as the unforgiving earth beneath it. I took another deep breath, my heart pounding in my chest and rolled the body over and I immediately recognized Cranough the elf, Darragh's proxy. His unseeing eyes were wide orbs of white in his face and there was an expression of shock on his mouth.

Beside him was what appeared to be some sort of puddling dark stain, like an oil slick. I stood up and tried to step around the puddle as I inspected it, all the while dawning realization spread through me.

When a grim perished, it didn't leave behind a body. It left behind an oily residue of its former self—the same oily residue I was looking at now. That meant both Darragh and his employee were... dead.

I gasped as the next thought to hit me was who in the world could have done this and, furthermore, were they still here? I decided not to find out. Instead, I made a hasty retreat back through the cemetery and to the 4Runner. Throwing open the door, I seated myself behind the wheel and immediately locked myself inside. Then I fought to catch my breath and talked myself out of bursting into a fit of tears. Tears weren't going to help me right now.

Instead, I pulled out my cell phone from inside my purse and dialed Taliyah Morgan, the new chief of police in Haven Hollow.

I felt the seconds tick by as the phone rang and rang and rang. When someone finally answered, I was so out of it, I wasn't even sure what they'd said or whether I'd even dialed the right number.

"I need to... I need to speak to Chief Morgan," I somehow managed.

"Who is calling?" the man responded.

"This is Seraphina Stenham," I replied.

"Fifi from the Half-Moon?"

"Right," I answered, barely even cognizant of the conversation.

"I haven't seen you working there in… at least two weeks? You got yourself another gig somewhere else?"

"Um… yeah," I managed, wishing the guy would just hand the phone over to Taliyah because I could barely think, let alone speak.

"So, what can I help you with?" he continued, not bothering to identify himself. Obviously, he thought I'd recognize his voice. I didn't.

"I… I need to speak to Taliyah," I said again, switching to her first name in hopes he'd think it was a personal call, but when he hesitated, I decided to make it obvious. "It's personal and it's important."

"Hold on a second."

I heard a clicking noise and was afraid he'd hung up on me, but then I heard a trilling sound as the line was transferred.

"This is Sheriff Morgan," Taliyah said as she picked up.

I didn't know what to say, and remained quiet for a few seconds.

"Hello?"

"I…" I started, my voice suddenly refusing to comply. "I… need to report a double homicide."

Chapter Eleven

"What is she doing?" I whispered, nervously.

"Pacing," Roy replied.

He, Poppy, and Marty had joined me at the police precinct where we were currently watching Taliyah walk back and forth, behind the glass walls of her office, speaking on the phone to someone.

It had been over three hours since I'd called in the double murder, and Taliyah had summoned me to the station. As soon as I'd gotten off the phone with Taliyah, I'd needed to talk to someone and noticing Poppy's house in the distance, I'd practically knocked her door down in my haste to speak with her.

Maybe I shouldn't have been surprised (owing to what Roy had said) to find that Marty was at her house too, about to sit down to dinner with Poppy and her son, Finn. Upon seeing me, I'm not sure which of us was more tongue-tied, Marty or me. But, I was fairly sure we both were the same shade of red.

Regardless, I was too discombobulated after discovering Darragh and Cranough were dead to feel jealous that Marty was visiting Poppy or to worry about coming face to face with Poppy after my kiss with Roy. Instead, I was just frantic to talk to someone. And, as was her way, Poppy immediately invited me in and as soon as I told her what happened (in the midst of a bout of tears), she gathered me into her arms and crooned into my ear that everything would be okay.

I wasn't sure when Roy had come into the picture—if Poppy had called him or if he'd called her. Either way, it was maybe thirty minutes later that I was sitting in Poppy's kitchen, nursing a cup of 'Calming Tea', when Roy came striding through her front door.

And when he'd seen Marty, he hadn't looked happy.

Luckily, everyone kept their disgruntled feelings to themselves, all of us focused on the larger context—that being the death of Darragh and his representative. After Marty had called to ask RJ and Henner to watch Finn and they'd agreed, the rest of us had headed to the precinct.

"She's fading," Poppy observed, from where she sat beside me, on one of the benches in the hall outside Taliyah's office. Marty sat on her other side. Roy, meanwhile, was doing a good job imitating Taliyah's pacing.

"Fading?" I repeated.

Poppy nodded. "Her hair used to be a rich sandy brown. Now, it's going silver."

Taliyah was probably close to my age, but an inch or so taller. She was leggy, but her police uniform didn't accentuate her hourglass figure very well. Just like Poppy had mentioned, at one point Taliyah had sandy brown hair artfully streaked with silver in places—and that silver had pretty much taken over now. Her eyes were sky blue, large with a fringe of long lashes and eyebrows that seemed naturally arching and narrow. Her doe eyes, pert nose and full lips were set in a delicate triangular face. She was definitely pretty and then some. But, she had the personality of a crocodile.

"Lots of people in stressful jobs get gray hair early," Marty replied with a shrug.

I smiled at him as I thought to myself how hopelessly human he was sometimes, despite knowing the truth about Haven Hollow and its monster inhabitants. Stress had nothing to do with why Taliyah was getting that silvery sheen to her hair. No, the silver hair was owing to the fact that she was heir to the throne of the Faerie Court of Winter. A powerful memory charm prevented her from remembering who she was. But, that memory charm was losing its strength with each passing day and the truth was making itself known little by little.

"The silver in her hair has nothing to do with Taliyah's stressful job," Poppy said with a little laugh as Marty gave her an expression that begged explanation. "She's heir to the throne of Winter, remember?"

"Ah, that's right," he answered with a quick nod. "But what does that have to do with gray hair?"

"It's not gray, it's silver," I corrected him, but he didn't even look at me. Instead, it was like he was transfixed by Poppy, as though he couldn't pull his attention away from her. And that realization weighed me down even more than I already was. Roy was right—Marty was head over heels for Poppy. I just didn't understand why I hadn't seen it before.

Why hadn't I seen it before?

I wasn't the only one who noticed either. When I looked up, I found Roy's attention fully focused on the two of them, and his jaw was tight.

"Hmm, you think I'll find out I have some supernatural heritage?" Marty asked Poppy with a beaming smile.

"No," Roy replied flatly. If he were a woman, I might have called his tone "catty". I glanced in his direction, one eyebrow raised, and he smiled at me sheepishly.

"I don't know," I started, returning my attention to Taliyah. "She could be stressed out. Don't forget, she's new to all this and still trying to wrap her head around the strangeness of Haven Hollow. Until recently, she probably thought supernatural creatures were just things in her nightmares."

"That's true," Poppy said. "She certainly didn't come here thinking she'd be dealing with mythological creatures, monsters even."

"Plus, it hasn't been that long since she lost her brother," Marty added. Yes, it had been a very sad day when Cain, Taliyah's brother and Marty's cousin, had been murdered.

"*Adopted* brother," Roy corrected her.

"A brother is a brother, Roy," Poppy replied, frowning at him. He just shrugged, but I noticed his eyes lingered on her.

"Fair enough."

We all watched as Taliyah hung up the phone and opened the door, motioning for us to enter. "This case is proving to be a nightmare," she said as she frowned at each of us in turn.

"How's that?" Marty asked.

"Killing an elf is a serious offense, but killing a grim is the equivalent of murdering an endangered species," she answered, still pacing. "The problem is… I can't rely on anything I've been trained to rely on."

"What do you mean?" Poppy asked.

"Human law is different to supernatural law, as you

know," she answered, finally sitting down at her desk as she threw her head into her hands and sighed. "And trying to walk the fine line between the two isn't easy." She looked up at me then. "Speaking of, when you called me, you didn't say anything about what happened to Darragh and Cranough to Deputy Sanchez, did you?"

I shook my head. We'd already been through this. "No, I just asked to speak to you."

"That's right, I already asked you that, didn't I?" I just nodded and gave her an understanding and sympathetic smile. She responded with another deep sigh.

"Luckily for us, I've managed to keep the crime scene on the down low, so the place isn't covered with forensics and detectives."

"That's a good thing," Marty said, before reaching over and patting her hand. "Just take deep breaths, Tally, we'll figure this out."

Taliyah nodded, but it didn't seem like she was acknowledging him—she looked like she was still lost in her own thoughts. "So, now I'm stuck with a dead elf and an oil slick that used to be a grim and I don't know what to do about either."

"Let the council handle it," Roy answered from the corner of the room, where he was towering over everyone else. "It's our jurisdiction, anyway."

Taliyah looked up at him and her eyes burned with fierce indignation. "This is *my* town, therefore it's *my* jurisdiction."

Roy just sighed and shook his head, like he wasn't interested in going up against her temper. Not that I blamed him—Taliyah's temper was becoming pretty legendary.

Taliyah turned back to the rest of us. "Usually I'd

91

order an autopsy if I had a dead body on my hands, but how am I supposed to do that when all my coroners are humans? Not to mention, I only have *one* body—the other is… dissolved."

"Regardless, the council should be included in this case," Roy said again.

"Why? You have someone who can explain the death of an elf and an oil slick that won't seep into the dirt?" Taliyah asked, glaring up at him.

"Not exactly," Roy answered.

"Do you even have paranormally inclined morticians on the council?" Poppy asked him.

He paused a moment too long. "Well, no."

"Then how is the council supposed to help me?" Taliyah continued.

Roy cocked his head to the side. "You have a point —those types of tests are beyond the scope of what the council can handle, but I still think they should be involved."

"You're on the council, aren't you?" Taliyah asked him pointedly. He nodded. "Then consider yourself involved." Then she looked at me. "What was protocol before I came here when a supernatural creature wound up dead?"

Protocol had been trying not to get Cain involved in supernatural affairs, but it wasn't as though I could say that to Taliyah.

"Protocol was… private," I started.

"Private?"

I cocked my head to the side, realizing I'd have to explain without explaining too much. "Whether or not the death was looked into… depended on what the families wanted." .

Taliyah frowned at me and started tapping her

fingernails against the desk like she was in a hurry and I was taking too much of her time. "What does that mean?"

"It means the way Haven Hollow handles supernatural deaths is to leave it up to the families of the deceased as to what they want to do with their dead," Roy answered in his concise sort of way.

"And if they wanted an autopsy?" she asked.

He nodded as if he was expecting her question. "If the family chooses to do an autopsy, then they have to find the coroner and order it themselves."

"So you don't have a police force to look into such things?" Taliyah asked, her eyes going wide.

"Not exactly," Roy answered. "Deaths of supernaturals are usually rare occasions anyway given that this is a Hollow and owing to our long life-spans, but when they do occur, they're handled by the surviving family members."

"The council doesn't get involved?" Poppy asked.

Roy looked at her, and his expression softened. "Only if the family asks us to. Usually, we just document the death, and whatever the reason for the death as mentioned from the family members and we leave it at that."

"That sounds very archaic to me," Taliyah said, and Poppy nodded in agreement.

"Has anyone notified Darragh or Cranough's next of kin?" Taliyah asked, as her gaze settled on me once again.

"Um," I started. "I doubt it because I don't think anyone in Haven Hollow knows their next of kin."

"This case just continues to spiral downwards," Taliyah responded.

"Seems to me like these deaths could be the work of

a hunter," Marty said, almost as an aside.

Just as there were monsters in the world, there were also hunters—humans determined and destined to hunt down all monsters and end them. That was one of the reasons why supernatural creatures rallied to Hollows— they were designated sanctuaries where those paranormally inclined could gather in numbers for protection. So, if this was the work of a hunter, that hunter had some serious guts to have come into a Hollow. But, I couldn't say my mind was fully concentrated on the idea of hunters coming calling to Haven Hollow. Instead, I couldn't stop thinking about the fact that this case could spell the end for Hallowed Homes.

The more I thought about it, the more I decided news about this situation could definitely have a bad impact on my new business—especially given the fact that Darragh had been actively working with us to find a graveyard. As soon as this story broke through the supernatural community, everyone would associate Hallowed Homes with dead elves and grims and that was a connection I wanted no part of.

I turned to Marty, hoping to find comfort in his smile or the kind word he always had at the ready, but as I looked up at him, his eyes were already engaged—on Poppy. A small smile adorned his face and if it hadn't dawned on me before that Marty was head over heels for my friend, it really dawned on me now. It was just… in the way he looked at her—the way he couldn't take his eyes off her—the way he hung on every word she said. I didn't think Roy was thrilled with the realization either —he was doing his best not to look at either of them and I felt for him.

"Well, I'm not about to let whoever did this get away with it," Taliyah said, pulling our attention back to her. "I'm still in charge of this town and it's still my responsibility to protect our citizens and visitors, regardless of what form they take." She nodded as she took a deep breath. "But, the first step is finding out whoever the hell did this."

"And you can't rely on human authorities," I reminded her.

"Right," she said.

"I have Fox Aspen's number," Poppy piped up then. "He'll be able to tell me if any hunters were dispatched to Haven Hollow recently."

"Fox Aspen?" Taliyah repeated, her tone one of confusion.

Fox Aspen was just another name the Prince of the Faerie Court of Autumn, Prince Reynard, assumed. But, Reynard wasn't just a prince—he was also a super-natural detective of sorts—going by the alias of Fox Aspen. Not only that, but Prince Reynard/ Fox was promised in marriage to Olwen, the faerie Taliyah would become when her transformation was complete. As soon as the spell on Taliyah finally broke away and she became Olwen, the heir to the Winter Court, Prince Reynard would wed her. With this marriage, peace would be declared between the two currently warring courts.

Why were the two courts warring? Because there had been a usurper to Olwen's throne and the Court of Winter called Janara. It had been a couple of months ago that Janara and her retinue had come to Haven Hollow, searching for Olwen/Taliyah. Once she located Taliyah, Janara planned to murder her (just like she'd done to Taliyah's parents).

In their attempts to locate Olwen/Taliyah, Janara and her cronies had kidnapped some of the local children, including Poppy's own son, Finn. They'd tried to use the kids as ransom in order to get their hands on Olwen/Taliyah, but it was poor planning on their part. A seer had told them about Taliyah becoming Olwen, but the seer had been off regarding her timeline. She was a year too early, and Taliyah hadn't yet begun to transform into Olwen. Now, Janara and her attendants were being held captive within a magic circle in the middle of a forest on the outskirts of town.

Everyone in the Hollow knew this—everyone except for Taliyah, that is. She was still in complete ignorance about what and who she would become.

"Yeah. Fox has an in with Jonathan Moses, the current leader of the Hunter's Guild of the Americas," Poppy explained.

"It sounds like this Fox Aspen person is aligned with the hunters, then? If not a hunter himself?" Taliyah asked, her expression suspicious.

"He's only aligned with himself," Poppy answered with a shrug. "Besides, Fox owes me a favor so I'm sure if I asked him to do a bit of snooping on our behalf, he'd oblige me."

"A favor?" Taliyah repeated, eyeing Poppy narrowly, suspicion still ripe in her gaze. But, Taliyah's lack of trust wasn't a slight against Poppy personally—it would have surprised me if Taliyah trusted anyone.

"I sort of saved his life," Poppy replied. "I'll give him a call tomorrow."

Taliyah exhaled the breath she'd been holding. "I guess it's as good a place to start as any. I'll work on a list of likely suspects, but first I need to do a more thorough examination of the graveyard, which I'll start at first light." Then she looked up at Roy. "Maybe I don't need to say it, but I'm not leaving the details of these deaths to Darragh and Cranough's family members, if we're able to actually locate said family members. Even if Haven Hollow doesn't have a standard protocol for dealing with these types of situations, I'm going to implement one." Then she paused as she faced each of us again. "I don't suppose any of you could find a coroner to examine the elf's body?"

"We could ask around town to see if anyone knows of someone," Poppy started, but Taliyah shook her head.

"We need to keep this news from breaking before I've got a handle on the case. That means, you can't alert any of our supernatural residents to what's going on."

"Then how are we supposed to find a coroner?" Marty asked.

Taliyah looked at him, and her lips were tight. "You're going to have to get creative, and that creativity would be best suited outside Haven Hollow town limits. I don't want this case leaving my office—not until we know more."

This was going to be a tough assignment.

"I'll see if I can find someone," I told her, eager to resolve the case before word started getting around that might affect Hallowed Homes. Maybe it might have seemed selfish or insensitive of me, but I wasn't thinking of myself. Mostly, I was thinking of all my employees and their families. If Hallowed Homes failed, that would mean I'd not only failed myself, but I'd also failed them and that was a thought I just couldn't face.

"Alright. Let's adjourn for now and report back any news as soon as you have it," Taliyah said, as she turned to face Roy. "I'll need your help to retrieve the bodies. Well… the *body*."

"No problem," Roy answered.

"I can help too," Marty offered, but Roy nearly

interrupted him with a deep growl.

"I've got it covered."

Taliyah nodded and then stood up, showing us the door.

***

As we went our separate ways, gloom surrounded me and that gloom just doubled at the thought of trudging back to the house I was currently sharing with Angelo. I had so much to deal with, so much that was already plaguing me, and Angelo was the last person I wanted to add to the list.

"Hey, Fifi!" I heard Roy call as he approached me, sprinting to catch up. I stopped and waited for him. "Where are you headed?"

"Home, not that I'm excited to see Angelo," I grumbled, shaking my head.

Roy nodded, and it seemed his thoughts were causing him some distraction. "You could always stay at my place."

I looked over at him and frowned, surprised and guarded all at the same time. My expression must have revealed as much because Roy instantly started chuckling and held up his hands in a surrendering sort of way.

"I'm not propositioning you, Fifi," he started. "I'm just well aware of how Angelo is and we both know he'll only bring you further down. And you definitely don't need that right now."

"That's true."

"So… I'm just saying you could stay at my place, *as a friend*. I'll happily sleep on the sofa."

"I thought you had to help Taliyah?"

"I do," he answered as he reached inside his pocket and produced a ring of keys. He took one of them off and handed it to me. "Here you go."

Even though I was surprised (owing to what had happened between us earlier with the kiss and then Roy's less-than-thrilled response) the desire to avoid Angelo was enough that I accepted Roy's house key. But, not before promising myself nothing would happen tonight—no kissing, no touching, not even any hand holding.

Roy and I were friends and friends we'd stay.

Chapter Twelve

When Roy walked through his front door, after a couple of hours since giving me his key, we both were fairly quiet, almost uncomfortable. The sun was just starting to come up and although I'd been awake all night, I couldn't sleep. I just... wasn't tired.

Roy walked over to the couch, where I was sitting and previously staring off into space, and offered me a smile. "You want me to light a fire? It's a little cold in here."

"Sure."

I watched him lean over and hoist a large log that had been sitting beside the fireplace onto the grate and then he shoved a few handfuls of pine needles underneath it, to serve as kindling. As he did so, the muscles of his torso strained against his shirt and it was all I could do not to notice them. But, notice them I did because they were just so... large. Just like the man himself.

Roy lit a couple of matches, introducing them to the kindling surrounding the large log and the fire roared up, spitting and popping as soon as it made contact with the pine kindling. Roy leaned back on his haunches, his back still facing me, then apparently content with the state of the fire, stood up and turned to me with another handsome smile.

"It should warm up in here pretty soon."

I just nodded, not really in the mood to talk. To his credit, he didn't try to force conversation. No doubt he knew how devastating this whole Darragh situation was for me. What he didn't know was how much it had wrecked me to watch Marty looking all moony-eyed at Poppy. Not only was I jealous and envious, but I also felt stupid. When Marty had come to the office to drop off his gift, it hadn't been because he had ulterior motives. He'd just come to see me as a friend and that realization stung. And then I'd gone and stuck my foot in my mouth when I'd asked him out to dinner.

Oh, demons below, that's right—*I'd asked him to dinner*.

Regarding the subject of Poppy and Marty, I was more than sure Roy had his own feelings. Maybe that was why he'd invited me over—maybe he just didn't want to be alone with his thoughts?

"Do you want anything to eat or drink?" he asked.

"No, thanks," I answered, suddenly feeling sick to my stomach. "I should... I should probably try to get some sleep."

He nodded. "Make yourself at home—I think you know where the bedroom is?" He motioned down the hall, apparently just in case I forgot.

"Thanks, Roy," I said as I stood up.

"Sure. And if you need something to sleep in—my t-shirts are in the third drawer down."

"I appreciate it," I said in a small voice as all the events of late started to rain down on me and I felt beyond exhausted, despair circling overhead like a buzzard waiting to devour me.

***

It took me forever to fall asleep, my mind running in circles as I considered the ramifications of what had happened at Hollow Cemetery and what the deaths might mean for Hallowed Homes and my employees.

There was no way to know what had really happened—who had killed Darragh and Cranough and why. I also couldn't help but wonder if there was some sort of message behind the deaths? Even though I was sure it was just another instance of my imagination on overdrive, I found myself wondering what killing two innocent creatures meant? Could there have been any significance to the fact that they'd been murdered while looking at one of our property listings? Was there any way this murder could have been a message aimed at me? A warning?

Or were their deaths just random, and they didn't mean anything at all? I had no enemies—well, at least none I was aware of, unless one counted Angelo. While that might have sounded like a stretch, sometimes it definitely felt like we were more like enemies than siblings. But would Angelo have done such a horrible thing?

No, I couldn't believe that of him. Yes, he was petty and jealous, but he wasn't diabolical enough to kill two innocent creatures just to spite me. For as awful as Angelo was, I couldn't believe he'd kill *anyone* intentionally. He just… didn't have that level of malevolence in him. Even as an incubus, stealing people's life force—he'd never killed anyone.

That was one reason I couldn't sleep. The other reason happened to be sleeping in the living room. Knowing Roy was just a room away was driving my succubus up the wall. It was a shame the succubus had witnessed his bulging muscles when he'd made the fire, because now that was the only thing she could think about. Well, that and the kiss we'd shared.

My libido was running rampant even as I tried to push the memory of Roy's delectable body out of my mind or the taste of his lips when I'd... when *the succubus* had kissed him. Between my angst and her lust, I was having a hard time falling asleep, but finally managed to drift off for what felt like mere minutes, before daylight flooded the room.

***

"Ah, Sleeping Beauty has awoken," Roy said cheerfully as I tumbled into the kitchen. He was busily breaking a few eggs into a bowl and there was something already cooking on the stovetop.

Now that I wasn't in such a hurry to leave his house, I was able to get a better look at his accommodations, which were still decidedly small and drab. The living room, kitchen, and dining room were all adjoined in one open plan. The only other rooms in the house were his bedroom and a bathroom in the hall between the two. As I'd noted earlier, everything was some shade of brown with a bit of green thrown in here and there. I had to wonder if Roy had no sense of decor or if this was just what appealed to his sasquatch nature. Maybe his living area was meant to mimic the open forest. At least it was clean—spotless, in fact.

"I guess this place doesn't look exactly inviting,

huh?" he asked, no doubt noting my examination of the place.

"I think it's very… you," I answered on a smile.

He smiled in return. "Poppy didn't like it—she said it was too sparse and didn't look lived in."

I laughed. "I kind of agree with her."

"Hmm," he said as he paused in whisking the eggs and looked around himself. "You think I should brighten it up?"

"Only if you want to."

He shrugged. "I don't really notice stuff like that. I didn't grow up with a lot of fancy things. You've seen my village, so you know sasquatches live very simple lives without much clutter."

I nodded as I remembered the particulars. When I'd visited his family compound, it hadn't been for fun. Instead, I'd been fleeing Haven Hollow because Angelo had covered me in *Love's Goddess* potion, which had basically tripled the allure of my already prodigious pheromones until all the men (and some women) in town had actually come after me.

"I do like some of the more modern features of this place, though," Roy continued.

"I think your idea of modern and mine may be different," I laughed as I looked around myself, shaking my head. "I don't think I saw a television anywhere?"

He shook his head. "I prefer to read." He motioned to a bookshelf built into one side of the living room. It held an extensive collection of leather-bound books that looked like they belonged in some English manor house, not this little cabin.

"At least you have a phone."

"Yes. That's almost a necessity, though, isn't it?"

"I would say so," I laughed, glancing down to watch

him flip a few pancakes I hadn't even realized he was cooking. That was when I remembered I hadn't brushed my hair, my teeth or even looked in the mirror yet. I frowned down at myself, taking stock of his oversized black t-shirt which ended below my knees and my long, white socks which were bunched around my ankles.

Now that I'd joined the land of the living, I began to take in the view before me. Or, I should say, the succubus started to take in the view before her and when she did, she wasn't disappointed. Roy was naked, save for a pair of navy blue boxers. As he flipped over the pancakes on a cast iron griddle atop the stove, the muscles in his shoulders and upper back shifted and I had a hell of a time trying not to stare.

Don't gawk, Fifi!

The only words the succubus could think in response were something along the lines of how she'd like to climb him like a California Redwood, but not wanting to entertain such thoughts, I reminded her that Roy was my good friend, Poppy's ex and he was still hung up on her. And I tried to further lecture her that friendships last but relationships rarely do, at least for me. Much to the succubus' regret, I wouldn't ruin my friendship with Roy and I definitely wouldn't ruin my friendship with Poppy over a man—even a sexy, virile, handsome one like Roy.

Not that he was interested in me, anyway, because he wasn't.

"Do you like pancakes?" he asked, his voice interrupting my inner tirade. "I forgot to ask."

"Sure. Who doesn't like pancakes?" I was still having trouble tearing my gaze away from his muscular torso and that happy trail of hair wandering down across his rock-hard abs into his boxers…

Ugh.

"You okay, Fifi?" he asked, setting out two plates on the breakfast counter before piling each of them with a stack of blueberry pancakes, bacon and scrambled eggs.

"Huh?"

"Are. You. Okay?" he said more slowly.

"Oh. Yeah, I'm fine."

"It seems like there's something on your mind," he answered as he seemed to finally realize I was having a hell of a time trying to take my eyes off him. He glanced down at himself and cleared his throat, as if only now realizing he was half naked and his body was littered with muscles that weren't easy on an abstinent woman.

"Oh…" He started and then cleared his throat again. "I guess I should put on a shirt. Sorry."

"It's okay," I said as I glanced down at my food. "It's just… hard sometimes to fight against my nature and it's been… five years since I…"

"It's okay," he interrupted. "You don't have to explain to me. I get it."

I nodded as he offered me a kind smile. "I tend to run hot at night and so I only sleep in my boxers… I guess I just sort of forgot to get dressed this morning."

"You don't owe me any explanations, Roy. This is your house. You can dress, or *not dress*, however you want." Even though my words might have made me sound like I was in control of myself and the situation, I wasn't. Instead, I was blushing like a fool.

"I'll be right back," he said, disappearing into the bedroom and returning a moment later wearing a t-shirt that read 'Believe in Yourself'. Below the words was an image of a sasquatch. I laughed as he opened the fridge and bringing out a carton of orange juice, poured us both a glass.

"Nice shirt," I said.

"Thanks. I saw it at one of the tourist shops and couldn't resist." I didn't respond, so he continued. "So… What's on your agenda for the day?"

At the mention of my day, I deflated a little. "I'm going to try to get into the office early to call my parents."

"Your parents?"

I nodded. "Mom and Dad are pretty well connected with most supernatural communities, so I'm hoping they might be able to tell me where I can find a coroner or a mortician outside of Haven Hollow who can help us with Darragh and Cranough."

"Sounds like a good plan. I was able to get a sample of Darragh's remains when I was helping Taliyah with Cranough's body last night, so when you do find someone—we're ready on our end."

"Oh, good." An uncomfortable silence descended on us and we both just looked at each other awkwardly, before facing our plates and swallowing the silence with orange juice and breakfast. "These pancakes are amazing, by the way."

"Glad you like them. What else do you have going for today?" he asked, finishing off his bacon. I hadn't even touched mine.

"We have a couple of people coming in to look at houses and I need to advertise the tomb now that I've lost Darragh as my potential buyer."

"Human clients?"

"Some of them, for the houses anyway."

"And the tomb?"

I laughed at the question because it was obvious a human wouldn't be interested in buying a tomb—at least not for a home. "I'm going to run an ad in the Haven

Hollow Gazette and hopefully I'll drum up some interest from a revenant, a ghoul, ogre, or something similar."

The Haven Hollow Gazette was a newspaper that was in circulation only for supernaturals. It had been enchanted to appear blank to any humans who encountered it. Not only did those paranormals in Haven Hollow receive it, but neighboring towns did too. It was pretty much my main form of advertising.

"I can't remember the last time Haven Hollow was home to a revenant or a ghoul," Roy answered as he chewed on a bite of pancake and egg.

"I'm trying to encourage exotics to take residence here… I think it would be good for businesses in general."

He nodded. "I think it's a great idea. The more of us there are in a hollow, the safer we are."

"Right. Hopefully, it won't take too long to find someone interested in seeing the tomb."

He loaded his mouth with another bite and then covered his chewing with his enormous hand as he continued, "Just remember, we can't let any information about what happened get out."

I nodded. I remembered Taliyah's warning.

"I need to get going," I told him after another few seconds of silence.

"I guess we both do," he replied, standing up and walking around the counter as he took both our plates. I noticed he'd cleaned his, and I'd only nibbled at mine. Usually, I had a healthy appetite.

"Thanks again for everything, Roy," I said as I started for the front door. I had to go home so I could shower and get ready for work and the morning was already passing me by.

"Fifi?" he called out as I gripped the doorknob. I

turned back to face him and found him frowning at me. "You going to leave like that?" he asked as he pointed at me with his index finger, waving it slowly up and down.

I glanced down, realizing I was still wearing his t-shirt and no shoes. "Oh," I said and laughed. "Right."

I moved past him and walked into the bedroom to put on my own clothes from the night before, grumbling under my breath at my own stupidity. Roy must have thought I was losing my mind—talk about embarrassing. Lacking a brush, I ran my fingers through my hair and headed back out again, at least looking somewhat more presentable.

"Okay. *Now*, I'm leaving."

"Okay," he said, laughing. "Good luck with all the things on your list today."

I had a feeling I was going to need it.

Chapter Thirteen

Once arriving home, I skipped showering because I was running late and changed clothes in record time, all the while hoping Angelo wouldn't walk through the front door. I'd remained lucky so far this morning as there was no sign of him. No doubt he'd found some poor woman to spend the night with and was probably feeding on her this very moment.

Once settled into my office, I picked up the phone and called my mother, Desdemona. Dread filled me the moment the phone started ringing. It was never a good conversation with my mother, but this one was neces-sary, all the same. We needed to find someone who could run an autopsy on Cranough and run some tests on Darragh—or what was left of him.

My mother was also a succubus, but she and I were nothing alike. Whereas I was a hopeless romantic, I didn't believe my mother possessed a romantic bone in her body. No, she viewed men as means to ends. The only reason she'd married my father was owing to the fact that her father had deemed it a good match. Arranged marriages weren't uncommon in the older order of supernaturals. Anyway, my mother had once lived among the elite members of New York society, feeding off them and making them amenable to whatever needs she had, and she still possessed that snooty sense of entitlement. People had lost their homes, marriages and fortunes at her whims, though my mother never felt an ounce of guilt—no, she'd reveled in her own power. She still did.

"Seraphina, how nice of you to phone," she answered in that all-too-familiar, upper echelon, fake voice of hers. "It's been so long, I half forgot I even had a daughter."

"I'm sorry," I answered, hating the guilt trip I always suffered from her. Bea had told me more than once that I could choose to sever ties with my family, but I'd never been able to bring myself to do just that. Instead, I did my best to get along with them, even if doing so was a tall order. "I've just been... very busy."

"As are all of us, darling, as are all of us." She took a deep breath. "Your father and I just returned from the Caribbean. It was positively invigorating! I've never felt so alive. The people there are so generous and kind. Lovely people, really." I shuddered to think what she'd done to such lovely people.

"I'm glad you enjoyed yourself, Mom," I replied, playing my roll of polite listener until I could get a chance to talk about something more important. Conversations with my mother were always a process—first the guilt trip, then the long explanation of all the wild adventures she'd been having and then the reason why I was calling.

"I met an actual prince, Seraphina," she continued. There was nothing my mother enjoyed more than talking about herself and her exploits. "He was quite handsome and very wealthy. And he was completely smitten with me."

"Of course he was." All thanks to her succubus powers of seduction.

"I think the necklace he gave me might have hailed from the royal family's private collection. I'm quite certain I've seen it before in photos of the Queen, at any rate. How utterly fantastic is that, Seraphina?"

"Pretty fantastic."

"Who gets to own jewels that once belonged to a queen?"

"You, apparently." I did my best to hide my disgust. It did no good to get her dander up if I wanted her to cooperate. So, I let her prattle on for a good five minutes more before I finally had to stop her—simply because I couldn't take any more. Not to mention, my employees would be coming in soon and I needed to get information from Mom without being overheard by anyone in the office.

"Mom, listen," I said as soon as she paused to take a breath. "I need to ask you for a favor and then I have to get going because my employees will be here any minute."

"Of course. What do you need?"

I was fairly sure Mom wouldn't know any coroners, but she might know a doctor or two, and that would be a good place to start. "I need you to recommend a doctor outside of Haven Hollow who can deal with… paranormal creatures."

"That is quite a vague request, Seraphina." She took a deep, irritated breath. "And why don't you just see Dr. Greenscloth? As you're well aware, he treats all the paranormal in town."

"Right," I answered, and then hesitated. "But, this…

is sort of hush-hush, which is why I'm looking for a doctor *outside* of Haven Hollow."

"Hush-hush?" she asked, and I could tell she was exasperated with my lack of detail. "You know you don't have to keep secrets from me. What do you need a doctor for and why does it have to be hush-hush?" Then she paused. "Are you pregnant? You haven't been knocked-up by one of those dreadful yeti beasts, have you?"

I felt my mouth drop open. "No! Jeez, I'm not pregnant, Mom."

"Oh," she answered, and sounded strangely crest-fallen. "That's too bad."

Hmm, maybe this was a better angle to take, after all, I thought to myself. *Especially since I don't have another reason for asking for a doctor outside town limits.*

"Of course, it's good you aren't pregnant with a hairy abomination," Mom continued, "but I couldn't help but get excited thinking I may finally have my first grandchild." Ugh, this again. "You're running out of time, you know."

I rolled my eyes. Mom desperately wanted a grandchild to continue our family name. She didn't care if I was married or not, but she did care whether her grandchild was a pure-blooded incubus or succubus. Of course, as I got older and my fertility was on its way to becoming a thing of the past (I probably still had another couple of years left), Mom was getting closer to accepting any child I had, just as long as I had one. And Angelo was hopeless—as a quintessential womanizing bachelor, Mom knew she couldn't rely on him to settle down and start a family. So that only left me.

The sad truth was that she might never get a

grandchild at all—I mean, I couldn't even find a partner I wanted to have sex with! With each decade that passed, my chances of getting pregnant decreased. It was a part of the curse of being a succubus. My brother would remain fertile until the day he died. He could father a child on his death bed, while I'd lose my chance long before I hit what we considered 'old age'.

Regardless, this whole pregnancy angle might be the best way to get what I wanted from her. "I mean," I started, pausing for dramatic effect. "At least… I don't *think* I'm pregnant, but if I am… you know how gossip spreads in a small town."

"You don't *think* you're pregnant? Then that means there's a chance you are?"

"Well, I did miss my period, so I guess it's possible, but I… doubt it. I mean, I don't have any symptoms yet."

She laughed at that, just like I'd known she would. "Seraphina, you wouldn't have symptoms this early on, but missing your monthly bleeding is quite a big sign."

"Good point. Anyway," I continued with a faux sigh. "I'd really just like to get checked out. I mean… if I *am* pregnant, it would be good to… know… but, again, I'm trying to be private about this… matter."

"Of course, of course." She paused. "Oh, this is such delightful news!"

I took a deep breath and felt slightly guilty about this outright lie. If only she knew the truth—that I hadn't had sex in five years… It was almost comical. "Can you please just give me the names of some good doctors outside Haven Hollow?"

I figured even if the doctors she referred couldn't help with the autopsy, one of them might at least be able to refer me to someone who could. It was worth a shot anyway, even if I had to lie to her to get the information.

"I'll email you with a handful right now."

"Thanks, Mom," I replied before realizing I was talking to dead air—she'd already hung up. Hmm, the whole potential pregnancy had certainly gotten her into high gear.

"Tut tut tut," I heard someone admonishing me.

I turned around and found myself face-to-face with Angelo, a giant smirk plastered on his mouth. I wanted to smack it right off him.

"What do you want, Angelo?"

"You're a very bad girl… lying to our mother like that." He said the words in our native tongue—a language I hadn't used in years. I was surprised to hear it and then realized he was just further goading me—using our native language to drive home the point that I was breaking my mother's trust.

"I don't know what you mean."

"You aren't pregnant and, furthermore, you have no intention of getting pregnant, Fifi. More importantly, you have no opportunity."

"What are you talking about?"

"I'm talking about the fact that I know that little stunt you pulled with your stable of sasquatches was just for show." He narrowed his eyes as he studied me and walking further into my office, leaned against the wall and crossed one leg over the other, looking like he owned the place. "You're not feeding and I'm going to prove it."

"I'm feeding and I've *been* feeding," I insisted, glaring at him. "So there's nothing to prove."

"You haven't and I know as much because I've been keeping tabs on you."

Instantly, I felt a spire of anger well up within me—

who in the hell did he think he was? Keeping tabs on me? I stood up, not enjoying the feeling of him staring down at me. "You're stalking me?"

"I wouldn't use that word."

"Stalking and 'keeping tabs' on me are the same thing," I insisted as dawning realization overcame me. The reason he'd asked to stay with me while his floors were installed was because he wanted to snoop—he wanted to keep an eye on me to report back to my parents. "Why are you so pathetic?"

It was his turn to glare at me and in his expression was hatred. "I made the mistake the first time of not having proof that you were starving the succubus. I'll be better prepared next time."

"There won't be a next time because Mom and Dad are sick of you and everything you've been trying to pull where I'm concerned. And, furthermore, if you were really keeping tabs on me, then you'd know I'm feeding on Roy Osbourne!" I smiled as his expression dropped slightly, before his poker face was intact again. "In fact, I spent the night with him last night. But, since you've been keeping an eye on me, you already knew that, right?"

"How could I possibly have known that when the enormous oaf lives with the rest of his backwoods family in that village in the mountains?"

I smiled even more broadly. "Roy doesn't live in the mountains, Angelo. He lives right here in town, but as a… *detective*… you should have already known that."

"I don't believe it," he barked at me, stepping closer until I was forced to crane my neck upwards in order not to break eye contact with him.

"If you don't believe me, then smell me!" I insisted, suddenly beyond grateful I'd skipped showering this morning.

Angelo grabbed my arm hard and then leaned into me, sniffing me like some sort of animal sizing up its competition. I could see his eyes widen as he detected Roy's scent.

I raised one eyebrow and smirked back at him. "There. Are you satisfied now? Not that it's any of your damned business in the first place!"

"I won't be satisfied until you're back home in New York doing what you were born to do," he answered, wrapping his arms against his chest.

"And what's that?"

"Seducing politicians and billionaires—using your natural gifts to gain wealth and power for our family."

"I'm attaining wealth in a different way," I answered, stepping away from him. "And I'm doing it with my own talent and hard work."

Angelo shook his head and chuckled, but the sound was ugly. He looked around himself before his eyes settled back on me. "Do you really think you'll ever achieve anything worth a damn with this failing business of yours? Selling homes to exotics, Fifi? Really? There's a reason Ophelia didn't take on that market—because there isn't one."

"What I do is none of your concern," I spat the words back at him. "And let me remind you I'm also your employer and that means I can fire you."

"We both know you won't ever fire me, Fifi. You don't have the guts."

"Why don't you push me hard enough and find out?"

"Regardless, you're sullying our family name with your antics and that's something Mom and Dad won't abide," he said, starting to raise his voice. "I'm well aware that your biggest client ended up dead in the graveyard and that's likely just a taste of things to come."

"Shhhh!" I said immediately, not wanting any of my employees who were already piling in, to hear him. It was a split second later that my mouth dropped open as the realization of what he'd just admitted warred through me. Angelo knew about Darragh and Cranough? How was that possible? Unless... unless...

"Your first exotic client and now he's dead," Angelo continued in a loud voice, laughing.

Just then, a heavy crash came from outside my office, the sound of something shattering against the tile of the sales floor. We both froze for a moment before I pushed Angelo aside and stepped out my office door to find out what had happened. I noted the coffee pot shattered on the floor where Libby had dropped it, her face frozen in shock. Behind her, all my employees stood stock still, all of them staring at me.

"What do you mean, *dead*?" Glenn, the werewolf, asked.

"Darragh is dead?" Bea bleated.

I stood there, looking back at them, trying to gather my thoughts, trying to come up with some reasonable explanation for what Angelo had just said. All the while, Taliyah's warning to keep the case on the DL rattled through my already overwhelmed mind. But the more I racked my brain, searching for something to say, the emptier it became. And I couldn't stop the panic that suddenly visited me because the fact that Angelo knew what had happened meant that it was just a matter of days before the rest of Haven Hollow would find out.

Chapter Fourteen

"I know you have questions, but some of you also have appointments this morning and our clients are our first priority," I started, facing everyone as Angelo shook his head and, snickering, left my office. "Let's get our morning appointments over and done with and then we'll talk about everything over lunch—my treat," I finished, doing my best to attempt to calm them. Yes, I was breaking protocol, but I didn't think there was any way around it. They'd already heard Angelo say Darragh had been murdered. The truth was out, so now it was up to me to make sure that truth didn't get exaggerated into something else entirely. Taliyah would have to understand.

"Stalling anyone?" Angelo remarked from where he stood at the end of the hallway. I could almost feel the sarcasm dripping in his tone, as if it had taken on a thick physical presence.

The sound of his voice made the hairs along my arm stand up at angry attention. He was so infuriating, always doing whatever he could to sabotage me and my business. There was nothing he wanted more than to see me fail, so I'd be forced to return home and become like our mother, sucking the life out of anyone unfortunate enough to cross my path. But, that wasn't me and it never would be.

Yes, there were moments when I wanted to fire him, when I wanted to tell him we were through and I was no longer his sister… But, no matter how bad it got between the two of us, I could never bring myself to say the words. Maybe it was just stupidity on my part, but I still believed in family bonds, even if I wasn't close with my parents. Maybe that was all the more reason why I so desperately hoped things could be different with Angelo, that things could be better—because he really was the only family I had.

"You weren't even going to tell them what happened, were you?" he continued, glaring at me.

"You should shut up now, Angelo. You've done enough," I told him through gritted teeth, hidden by the smile I continued to maintain for the sake of my employees, who were still looking directly at me.

"Or I haven't done enough. It depends on who you ask."

I narrowed my eyes on him and realized this whole argument was going to get personal—it already had. It was just a shame it had to be in front of my employees. "I mean it, Angelo. I don't have time for your antics right now. Get out of the office and go do your job."

"As you wish, your Highness. Good luck," he laughed, sauntering out the front door.

I took a deep breath and let it out slowly. Then another. And another. Then I turned around and stalked back down the hallway until I reached my office. Throwing the door shut behind me, I sat back down at my desk as I tried to prepare myself emotionally for the conversation I'd been forced into having. A conversation that Taliyah wouldn't be happy about.

***

When we finally broke for lunch in the conference room, everyone was quiet as they took their seats around the large oval table, and Libby busied herself with unpacking our lunch which had just been delivered by a local Italian restaurant called 'Giseppe's'. Our lunch consisted of deli sandwiches, potato salad, coleslaw, chips, and brownies, with various Italian sodas.

Once everyone was seated and their lunches were spread out before them, I started explaining, "This information is confidential at this point in the case," I said as I looked at each person in turn. "And the only reason I'm telling you what happened and breaking my agreement with Taliyah is because I have no other choice."

It took me about ten minutes to explain, in detail, everything that had happened the night I was supposed to meet Darragh and Cranough at the graveyard. Everyone looked concerned, which wasn't surprising, but there was nothing I could do about their concern now.

"So, they were murdered?" Bea asked.

"It appears that way."

"Who would do something so horrible?" Ivan chimed in, looking distraught by the news. "Are there any leads yet?"

I shook my head.

"Are we safe?" Libby asked, her eyes wide.

"I think so."

"How can you possibly think any of us are safe with

a killer running around the Hollow?" Angelo demanded, a smirk still adorning his beautiful, yet diabolical, face. If ever there were a devil in disguise, it was Angelo.

"There's no reason to believe anyone other than Darragh and Cranough were the targets," I answered. "For all we know, they had their own enemies."

"Are you sure there's no way Hallowed Homes could be the target?" Libby asked, worrying her lower lip.

"There's no evidence that says any of this has anything to do with Hallowed Homes."

"There's also nothing to say it doesn't," Angelo added with a shrug.

I shot him a dirty look, but he only smiled more broadly as he put his feet up on the desk and began eating his sandwich. I ignored him and continued speaking to the others instead. "For now, I need you to try as best you can to put this out of your mind and focus on your clients. And I'm asking for your silence. If this gets out before we have more information about the killer or killers, it could muddy the case and cause hysteria in Haven Hollow."

"True," Ivan said.

"I say we all take a vow to keep this between us," Glenn continued.

"And not let it leave this room," Ramona added.

"Count me in," Libby said.

The others all chimed in and I tried not to let the tears that were already stinging my eyes show. "Thank you," I managed. "I appreciate it more than you know."

"Angelo?" Bea said as she faced my brother.

He shook his head. "You all can have your little vow, but I'm not interested."

"How did you happen to know about the murders

anyway?" Glenn asked, narrowing his eyes at Angelo.

"Yeah, isn't it a little... *convenient* that you happened to be at the graveyard at the same time the murders happened?" Ivan continued.

"If you'd like to know, I've been trailing my sister," Angelo started as I realized what he was about to tell them—that he was spying on me to prove to my parents that I wasn't feeding and hadn't been.

"That's enough," I interrupted. Then I faced everyone else in the room. "Ivan, Bea and Glenn all have open houses this afternoon... some into the night and I will have more listings shortly for Angelo and Ramona."

"Do you think Hallowed Homes might have to shut down because of... the murders?" Ramona asked.

I could understand her concern. As a wraith, it would be difficult for her to find employment in general. Like night hags, many wraiths could pass as human but only to an extent—night hags had the unfortunate habit of rotting plants and wraiths weren't much different— they both were bad for the landscape.

"We'll be fine, Ramona," I told her, giving her a big smile as I did my best to soothe her. "Everything will be okay."

Angelo laughed as I glared at him. "I hope the entire company sinks. Then we can go back home to New York and put this absurd idea of you being a land baron to rest."

"You put a lid on it!" Libby yelled at him, facing him with an ugly expression as she surprised the hell out of me. Bea gave me a look that said she was amazed as well.

"Yeah, we've all heard just about enough from you," Bea said as she faced my brother, crossing her arms against her chest as her wings suddenly fluttered out of her cape—revealing she was agitated.

"You are lucky your sister feels bad enough for you to offer you a position here," Libby continued, glaring at him. "Fifi has too big a heart to see what a lech you really are!"

"I second that," Ivan said.

I returned Angelo's petulant gaze, all the while wondering if he really did have anything to do with the deaths of Darragh and Cranough, like Ivan and Glenn had not so discreetly intimated. Of anyone, Angelo had the most motive to have killed my clients, because he only stood to gain if my business went under. But, I was still caught on one detail—would Angelo really take things that far? I didn't think so, but I also didn't know for sure. I didn't want to believe him capable of something so horrible, but the honest truth was that I didn't know what Angelo was capable of.

"I'm out," he said as he stood up and walking out of the conference room, slammed the door behind him.

I turned back to face my staff, who all looked uncomfortable and anxious despite my best efforts to calm them. I was sure Angelo's outburst didn't help things. But, that was something I couldn't focus on now —I'd handle it later. For now, I had to pay attention to my staff and hopefully alleviate any concerns they had.

***

After lunch, everyone began shuffling back towards their desks, still looking dejected and concerned. Some of them gathered closely together in the break room, whispering feverishly to one another as I wondered whether or not this whole situation would blow over.

It was then that Angelo decided to make another

appearance as he walked out of his cubicle and into the hallway, heading for my office. And that was just as well, because I was already on my way to his desk. I glared at him, my lips pursed together in a thin line as I spoke to him through gritted teeth.

"My office. Now!"

He followed me in, and I closed the door behind us, trying to maintain as much calm as I could, despite how angry I was. And my anger spoke volumes because, in general, I wasn't someone who lost her cool easily. Usually I was just laid back and easygoing Fifi. But, Angelo had a way of pulling the worst out of me.

"What do you want?" he growled.

"I don't appreciate you trying to upstage me in front of my employees. And I really don't appreciate the fact that you came out with the information about the murders before I have any answers. You put me in a position of trying to explain something I don't yet fully understand, not to mention the fact that this is police business and you shouldn't have mentioned it at all!" I took a deep breath. "All you do is undermine me and I'm sick of it."

"You should always be honest with your employ-ees," he responded with a dismissive shrug, glib as ever.

"This information wasn't supposed to get out yet," I responded.

"Someone killing supernaturals in town is something everyone should be aware of, especially if the murders somehow tie back to this office."

"And why would you think the murders have anything to do with Hallowed Homes?"

He frowned at me. "Oh, I don't know, Fifi, maybe because Darragh was murdered during one of your showings?"

125

"That could have been coincidental."

"And it might not have been coincidental."

I further narrowed my eyes at him. "For all I know, *you're* the one who's responsible."

"Responsible for what? Killing a grim and an elf?" He started chuckling when I didn't make any motion to deny the accusation. "I may be a lot of things, sister, but you really think I'm a killer?"

"I believe there's no limit to how far you'll stoop in order to ruin me."

"If you say so."

I could see the anger boiling beneath the surface. Angelo's biggest shortcoming was his pride and as such, he didn't like being questioned. I wasn't convinced he was the killer or that he even had it within him to kill someone, but he also wasn't opposed to doing someone harm. Furthermore, I didn't believe he was past draining someone's life essence to get his way. Maybe that's what he'd done in this case and he'd just gone too far? Anything was possible when it came to Angelo and his greed. He was just like our mother.

"While we're discussing this office, let me remind you that I own this business."

"So what?"

"So this is your last warning."

It took only seconds for his entire face to completely redden with anger. "I've heard enough," he muttered as he turned and yanked open the door, storming out. The staff all looked nervously at him as he passed by, but no one said anything. He bolted out the front door and disappeared down the street.

***

"I want to go with you," Bea said as she entered my office and noticed the sheet of paper in my hand—it was a list of doctors outside Haven Hollow I'd printed from my mother's email.

"I think it's best if you stay clear of this, Bea."

She crossed her arms against her chest and gave me that look of attitude only a faerie can. "I know you want to take all of this on your own back, but I'm not going to let you do that."

"Bea…"

"I want to help you, Fifi."

I frowned at her. "Helping me could mean putting yourself in danger."

"Since when have you known me to shy away from danger? Besides, I'm already involved."

I narrowed my eyes at her. "What do you mean, *you're already involved*?"

Her eyebrows reached for the ceiling as she inspected her fingernails, playing nonchalant. "I was just talking to Angelo and he told me the elf who was killed was a member of the Autumn Court."

Damn Angelo for running his mouth. Just then, a memory of Marty mentioning he thought Fox might be involved in the murders suddenly revisited me. Hmm, Fox Aspen was also the Prince of the Autumn Court. Coincidence?

"I have many friends in the Autumn Court," Bea continued.

"Did you know Cranough?"

"Well, no."

"Then?"

She plopped her hands on her hips and scowled at me. "I can't just stand by and let whoever did this get away with murdering one of my own." She took a deep breath. "I want to be involved." Then she paused for a moment and smiled up at me. "Besides, you know I can hold my own in a fight—I'm a good person to have at your back."

That part was true enough, although I didn't imagine I was going to be in any fights anytime soon. "They don't call you 'Kamikaze Bea' for nothing."

"That's right. I can dive bomb with the best of them."

"While that might be true, I really don't want to get you involved," I said, shaking my head. "If something happened to you..." Not to mention the fact that Taliyah would be pissed to know I'd brought Bea in. She was already upset when I'd showed up at her office with Poppy, Marty, and Roy in tow.

"I might be able to call in one of my unused tithes," Bea nearly interrupted. "This is the exact type of situation that would benefit from a favor."

"Who owes you a favor that could help me with this case?"

"Oh, just a coroner in Cherry Woods named Dr. Hedgewick."

Cherry Woods wasn't that far from Haven Hollow. I swallowed hard and Bea smiled broadly, realizing she'd just won because a coroner was just what the doctor ordered, no pun intended.

"I can give him a call right now," Bea continued. "And we could be at his doorstep in what? An hour?"

"Fine," I said as I picked up my list of doctor names and folding it, placed it in my purse even as I hoped I wouldn't need it.

"You'll be glad you let me help, Fifi, swear."

I looked at her and couldn't help but smile. "I guess another set of eyes can't hurt."

She nodded. "So what's our first order of business?"

"Are you finished with your appointments for the day?"

"Yes," she nodded as I breathed out a long sigh.

"Road trip!" she said gleefully. "I'll grab some snacks."

"No time."

"Okay," she nodded with one clipped motion. "Let's ride."

I left Ramona in charge of the office and Glenn with the responsibility of closing it. Then, Bea and I hurried out, on our way to the parking lot.

"Today is a great day to catch a killer," Bea said.

Chapter Fifteen

The good news was that I'd decided to bring the list of doctors with me because Bea had tried to call Dr. Hedgewick, the coroner, at least four times and hadn't been able to reach him. So we'd abandoned our plan of Cherry Woods and had headed into Portland instead.

The bad news was that each doctor we'd visited thus far were either gynecologists, obstetricians, and a few of them were even pediatricians—all basically useless for our needs. But, two of them had been helpful in referring us to other practitioners. Still, no one was able to help us with the type of forensic autopsy we needed.

"It's okay. Dr. Hedgewick will be able to help us, I'm sure," Bea chirped from beside me, ever the optimist.

"Um, the only problem is that you've called Hedgewick five times now and you still haven't been able to reach him."

"Maybe he changed his number. I say we just drive to his office and find out for ourselves," she answered and handed me a folded sheet of paper with an address scribbled across it. I looked at the address and realized

Dr. Hedgewick's office was fairly close—it was actually on our way back to Haven Hollow.

"Cherry Woods, here we come," I answered and starting the 4Runner, headed for the freeway.

It took maybe ten minutes before Bea told me to exit the freeway. Following her directions, we found ourselves on a long and twisting road that wound through nothing but miles and miles of cherry trees, no doubt the reason why the town had been named Cherry Woods.

"I think we take a right here," Bea said as she peered through the window and then nodded to me. I took the only turn I could—a right onto a single-lane road with nothing but cherry trees on either side, stretching for as far as the eye could see.

After a few miles, the trees gave way to open grassland, dotted here and there with a few cows.

"Are you sure this is right?" I asked. It just—didn't look like the type of place a coroner would set his business because it was in the middle of nowhere.

Bea nodded. "I mean… I'm pretty sure it's right. It's actually been a long time since I worked for Dr. Hedgewick."

"So… you basically have no idea where we're going, do you?"

"I wouldn't say it like that, exactly," she started, frowning as her lips broke into a big smile and she pointed straight ahead. "What's that?" she asked, sounding momentarily hopeful again as she motioned to the building ahead of us that appeared almost out of nowhere.

I looked at the small brick building that was one story tall and in the shape of a rectangle and pretty much nondescript, except for the fact that it was derelict and no longer inhabited, exemplified by the wooden boards that covered each window. It sat alone on the side of the road, nothing but open grassland on either side. As we approached, I slowed down until I could make out the large metal sign that stood beside the main entrance: "Eternal Bliss Charnel House."

I pulled to the side of the building and parked the SUV, turning off the engine as Bea looked at me and nodded.

"Yep, this is the place," she said, looking at the building through her window with a self-impressed smile. "Looks like my directions weren't wrong after all."

"Not that your directions really matter considering the place looks like it's been out of business for a long time. No wonder Dr. Hedgewick wasn't returning your calls."

"Hmm," Bea answered while she chewed on her lip and I sighed out my frustration as I continued to inspect the old building. Bea, meanwhile, opened her door and jumped down to the concrete sidewalk that appeared just in front of the building.

I followed suit, even though I wasn't sure why we were even getting out—Hedgewick clearly wasn't here any longer and probably hadn't been for some time.

"When did you work for Hedgewick? How long ago?"

She shrugged. "At least ten years."

I nodded, because the shape of the building made it seem like it had sat empty for at least ten years, easy. "Looks like Hedgewick ran out on the tithe he owed you."

"I just… hmm… I wouldn't have thought he was the type," Bea answered, shaking her head.

"What was this place doing out in the middle of nowhere in the first place?"

She shrugged. "Hedgewick is a weremole and only worked on paranormals... so I guess it makes sense that he'd want to keep his business out of the reach of mundanes."

"A weremole?" I repeated, frowning. "I didn't know there even were such things."

"Yep, there are."

Bea started forward, while I continued to inspect the boards on the windows, trying not to get disappointed by the way this day had gone.

"Did you see that?" she asked, pulling my attention to her wide eyes.

"See what?"

There was the definite expression of shock on her face. "I'm pretty sure I just saw a brownie trying to break into the back door, over there." Then she pointed to the back door in question, which was on the side of the building. From this vantage point, I couldn't see much.

Brownies were another sect of the fae and were typically of or related to the home. They were pint-sized creatures that were generally fair-tempered, though they could be provoked to anger and then they were a nasty little bunch.

"A brownie?" I asked her, frowning. It was highly unlikely to randomly spot a brownie in the daytime, away from its home—especially out here, in the middle of nowhere. They were notoriously private creatures who lived isolated lives. "Why would a brownie break into this place? Aren't they supposed to protect houses?"

Bea nodded. "I don't know why, but I'm sure that's what I just saw."

Hmm, maybe the little creature was in trouble and needed help. As we approached the end of the wall of the building, I peered around the corner and watched as the brownie climbed up a pile of refuse and removed a few loose boards from one of the windows.

Owing to his earth toned and ratty clothing, he appeared to be what was known as a *Domovoi* from the Autumn Court, and he was definitely a brownie—as decided by his diminutive stature (he was maybe two feet tall on a good day). He had long and skinny arms and legs and a round, pudgy middle. His reddish hair was scraggly, sticking out underneath his knitted green cap, which did little to disguise his massive nose and round, orb-like eyes.

The brownie gripped the sides of the remaining boards, slipped through the opening and disappeared, having never spotted us.

I hurried up to the door, but when I tried to pull on the handle, it was apparent it was locked from the inside. That left only the window, one of the boards of which was already missing, owing to the brownie removing it.

"I can see him through the window," Bea said as she stood on her tiptoes and looked up at the window, then pulled back to take stock of the boards that still remained. "I'm pretty sure I can fit through."

"Go!" I encouraged her as her wings suddenly unfolded from her back, poking out from underneath her velvet cape, and she floated up to the window. Once she reached it, she grasped each side of the wooden boards that covered the window and then squeezed through the narrow opening.

"Be careful," I whispered.

Once on the other side, I watched her float down to the concrete floor below as she hurried to unlock the door and I met her on the other side.

When I stepped foot inside the building, I shivered with the dank cold and my eyes fought to accustom themselves to the dark. The large windows that sat to one side of the door were all painted black on the inside and boarded up on the outside. Other than the broken one Bea had just climbed through, we were left with little light filtering in from outside, and with dusk approaching, that wasn't much light to begin with.

I looked around as my eyes adjusted to the darkness, but saw nothing. No doubt the brownie had definitely seen us coming, and he'd taken refuge somewhere. Not that that was very surprising. As I'd mentioned, brownies were solitary creatures and even if one were in trouble, he wouldn't just welcome the interference of others. I scanned the room again and leaned in toward Bea.

"Can you see anything?"

"No. He's hiding," she whispered.

I pulled my phone out of my pocket and turned on the flashlight app. The room around us began to glow and revealed itself to be in pristine condition—and it was definitely a mortician's office, with polished tables and instruments laid out on a side table, waiting for sterilization and use. Strangely enough, the room looked like it was in use—the instruments were shiny, there was no dust or cobwebs anywhere. Hmm…

There was a side alcove hidden behind the wall's shadow. Had the brownie hidden in there? I walked slowly toward the alcove, panning my phone this way and that, looking for signs of the little creature, but there was nothing aside from a row of cabinets.

It was possible the brownie had gone through the nearby double doors—which, based on their proximity to the exam area, I assumed was a cold storage for bodies. A shudder ran through me as I contemplated having to enter the room to look for him. I just… didn't like the subject of death in general—it gave me the heebie jeebies.

"I think he went in there," I said and pointed to the double doors.

"Lock and load, baby," she quipped, heading toward the doors.

Inside, the room was empty other than a row of three metal preparation tables and the instruments required for embalming and funeral presentation. Unlike the orderly and tidy room outside, this room was dusty and appeared to be as derelict as the building that housed it. It was also far too warm to be a cold room.

"What's a brownie doing here?" I whispered, as I turned to face her.

"I don't know."

It was a perplexing mystery and one that was starting to appear unsolvable. Not yet wanting to give up, I walked toward a wall of small, metal doors where bodies would once have been stored. Figuring our brownie could be hiding within one of them, I started pulling them open, one by one. As I approached the middle section, I noted that one of the doors was ever so slightly ajar. I motioned to Bea, and she walked up to it, slowly reaching for the handle as she yanked it open in one fluid motion while I shined the light inside.

The brownie stared back at us, wide-eyed, as he cowered in the center of the body tray within. I prepared for him to shift into any type of animal form, or go completely invisible, but instead he screamed.

"It's okay," Bea crooned as I pulled back, allowing her to take the lead. He'd be less afraid coming face to face with one of his own kind than he would facing a demoness.

"We aren't going to hurt you," Bea said. "My name is Bumble Bee and I'm a faerie from the Spring Court."

"I know what you are," the creature said in a tinny, high-pitched voice, I imagined an alien might sound like.

"What's your name?" Bea continued.

"Me name is Burian."

"Nice to meet you, Burian," she said with a big smile. Burian didn't return it.

"What you want?"

"We just want to ask for your help," she responded.

"I can't help you."

Bea frowned but kept her Glinda, the Good Witch impersonation going. "How do you know? We haven't even told you what we need help with yet."

"I don't know you. Go away."

"Not until you talk to us, just for a bit and then we'll let you get on with whatever it is you're doing here."

It seemed like an eternity as we sat there looking at him, waiting for a response. Finally, he climbed out of the metal drawer and hopped onto a nearby exam table to face us, looking resigned.

I couldn't help but note how he continued to shiver, even after climbing out of the drawer where he'd been cowering in the corner, trying to hide from us by slipping into the shadows. "I'm not doing nothing wrong. I'm just watching the building I was assigned."

Hmm, brownies weren't usually assigned to buildings.

"Then why were you trying to break in?" I demanded, getting closer so I was right in his face.

"I didn't break in!" he insisted, shaking his head in quick succession. "I just forgot me key!"

I figured his story could be the truth, because there really was no reason for him to want to break into this place—not unless he belonged here. "You said you were assigned to this building. Assigned by whom? Who gave you the keys?"

"The prince himself, Reynard."

"The ruler of the Autumn Court?" Bea asked, surprised.

"Aye," Burian said with a clipped nod. "This location been me assignment for the last four years."

Hmm, Prince Reynard... AKA Fox Aspen—the detective Poppy had mentioned earlier—the one who owed her a favor.

"Why were you sent here?" Bea asked.

"To watch the mortician to learn his trade."

"Dr. Hedgewick?" Bea asked.

If Burian was surprised Bea knew the doctor, he didn't show it. Instead, he just nodded.

"Is Dr. Hedgewick still here?" Bea asked.

Burian shook his head. "He left long ago." He took a breath. "There, I've told you what you asked. Now tell me what you want."

I stepped forward because Burian had been looking at me—probably because I hadn't yet introduced myself. "I'm Seraphina Stenham and this is my employee, Bea. We're from Hallowed Homes. We were looking Dr. Hedgewick because he owes Bea a tithe."

"Well, he ain't here no longer," Burian answered.

"Where did he go?" Bea asked.

"I ain't know for sure."

"Why does Prince Reynard need a brownie mortician?" I asked, finding the whole situation completely bizarre. Clearly, whatever was going on here was on the down low—why else would Reynard have kept Burian secreted away in this derelict building in the middle of nowhere? The answer was obvious: because Reynard didn't want anyone to find out what he was up to.

Burian turned his gaze to me. "All's I know is the prince hired me for the job."

I faced Bea with a big smile, as I pushed the mystery of why Reynard was interested in autopsies aside, before looking at Burian again. "Then you're an actual coroner?" I questioned. "Able to dissect a supernatural creature and figure out the way in which he or she died?"

"Aye."

I smiled even more broadly. We might be in luck here, after all. It would seem Burian might be just the creature we needed to serve as a makeshift medical examiner for our dead elf and the remains of the grim.

Chapter Sixteen

"I need you to come with us to Haven Hollow," I told Burian, because I was fairly sure Taliyah wouldn't part with Cranough's body anytime soon. Better to try to bring Burian to her than bring Cranough to him.

"Absolutely not," Burian answered, wrapping his arms against his chest as he shook his head vehemently. "I can't leave this place. I'm nae allowed."

"This is important," Bea started as I wondered if maybe we *could* get Cranough's body to Burian somehow. Would Taliyah allow it? I wasn't sure.

"We need you to look at the body of a deceased elf," I continued.

"An elf?" The creature asked as it eyed me narrowly. "From which court?"

This was a subject on which I wasn't sure how he'd react. "The Autumn Court," Bea answered, and Burian's eyes went wider.

"What happened to this elf?" he continued.

"Someone murdered him and the grim he accompanied," Bea answered.

"What his name?"

"Cranough," I answered, watching him carefully, but there was no recognition in Burian's face. "We're trying to locate a mortician who can examine him…" I continued. "We need an autopsy."

Then Bea and I turned our hopeful expressions to Burian as he took a step back, continuing to shake his head. "Nae. Nae. Nae me. Me can't help you… even if Me wanted to."

"And why's that?" I grumbled.

Burian looked at me. "Me responsibilities are to the Prince only—an' sealed by oath."

"Can't you talk to him and explain we need your help?" I asked. "I'm sure once he hears the deceased elf is from the Autumn Court, he'll be interested in finding out more."

"No," Burian insisted. "Reynard wouldn't like it that I've talked with you at all, and me don't care to make him angry. Now leave me be."

I stood there looking at him, completely surprised he wasn't willing to help us, considering the dead elf was one of his own. I could understand if he didn't want to help if the elf were from another court (the various faerie courts were all in rivalry with one another), but this seemed highly suspect, not to mention odd.

Then something occurred to me—could one of the rival courts be responsible for the death of Cranough and Darragh? As soon as the thought birthed itself, I released it because it didn't make enough sense. Cranough hadn't been a high-ranking member of the Autumn Court. He'd been just another proxy, and I didn't imagine his murder would matter enough to the Autumn Court, as awful as that sounded. Not to mention, faerie courts tended to keep their disagreements with one another to themselves —and they never would have killed Darragh, not wanting to involve outside paranormal creatures. So, no, there was no motive for another court to have killed Cranough.

"Listen," Bea pleaded with Burian. "I know we're not from the same court, you and I, but we're all bound together by a common fae thread. And Cranough was from your court."

"So what?"

"So, we really need your help with this, and I don't know who else we can ask for such a favor."

"Me loyalty to Prince Reynard be more important than me helpin' you."

Bea sighed, but nodded all the same. The fae didn't break their word to someone, no matter *how* that word was secured. Whether given by choice or by coercion, it resulted in the same outcome—a fae's word would not be broken. Asking Burian to do something that conflicted with an oath to Reynard was a hopeless situation.

"I have some tithes I could give you," Bea continued as Burian looked at her with a spark of interest lighting up his eyes. "Some are quite lucrative," she continued. "I think I could make it worth your while and the prince need never know about our arrangement."

"Tithes? What sort of tithes?"

"What is it you'd like? I'm sure I have something that could be helpful to you," Bea said.

"Hmm…" Burian answered as he looked up at Bea and tapped his long, skinny fingers on his chin. "Mayhap I could coax the prince into considering your request if them tithes could benefit him."

Bea and I exchanged a brief look. Burian was thinking about the trade, clearly, but was it a good idea to give her tithes to the prince when she had no idea what he'd use them for?

"No," Bea said as she shook her head. "I don't want anyone else in on this trade. The tithes would be for *you* to use when *you* need them. They would have to be private, from one fae to another. Our secret."

"Me can't keep secret from the prince," Burian said, frowning up at her. "You know 'tis not in our nature to betray our masters."

Bea sighed loudly and shrugged at me, as if to say she'd tried.

No amount of coaxing was going to change Burian's mind, clearly, so we finally gave up and left him to his work, returning to the 4Runner to make the long drive home. I felt exhausted and disappointed after spending all day searching, only to end up with nothing at all.

Once we were seated inside the SUV and I'd turned on the engine, I took out my phone and hit Taliyah's contact info, watching as the call connected. I'd have to let her know about our progress, or lack thereof.

"What a waste of a day," I said on a sigh as I glanced sideways at Bea. She seemed equally disenchanted with this entire endeavor.

"Fifi, is that you?" Taliyah asked when she picked up the line.

"Yep," I answered.

"Well? What did you find out for me?"

I sighed, long and hard. "We didn't get much. The doctors on my mother's list were dead-ends, but along the way, we did come across a brownie, who appeared to be breaking into a building."

"Hmm, do I need to get involved in that?"

"No," I answered quickly—Taliyah getting involved in whatever was happening between Burian and Reynard was the last thing I wanted—especially because I was fairly sure Reynard didn't know Taliyah was back in Haven Hollow. As far as he knew, she was still in Portland and still under the magic keeping her ignorant to her true self. The only reason Taliyah had come to Haven Hollow was to help care for her ailing brother, Cain, before he'd died. And then she'd stayed on to look into his murder. "The point is, we asked for Burian's help because he was actually an... aspiring mortician, but he refused to help."

"Ugh, the little bastard!"

"Right," I answered. "I'm hoping maybe we can take up the cause with Reynard, but I wouldn't be surprised if he demands the remains of Cranough, because Cranough is from his court."

"Cranough died in Haven Hollow, which is my—" Taliyah started, but I interrupted her.

"Your jurisdiction, I know, but the supernatural community doesn't work like the human one does and all I'm saying is that if we want Reynard to work with us, we might have to work with him." I took a deep breath. I couldn't come out and tell her Reynard was her intended, and she was heir to the Court of Winter because it wasn't my place. But, I also didn't think it was a good idea for Reynard to know she was in Haven Hollow, because who knew what would happen then? Maybe he'd try to force her hand before she was ready? He was a prince, and he was unpredictable, so I figured it was best for Taliyah to lay low.

"Anyway, we're headed back," I continued.

"Thanks for doing what you did," Taliyah answered. "And I'll consider your request."

We said our goodbyes, and I disconnected the call.

"I'm hungry," Bea said as she turned to look at me. "Are you hungry?"

I nodded. "I could eat."

So, we stopped off at a little Mom-N-Pop diner along the highway for dinner. Bea ordered a salad with over ten different vegetables and I ordered a decidedly unhealthy cheeseburger and fries. This was at least one benefit to my being a succubus—I could eat whatever I wanted without worrying about gaining weight or the adverse health effects. Any excess weight just burned off, owing to my extremely high metabolism. That extremely high metabolism was also one of the reasons why I needed to drain so much energy from my lovers.

"Do you think that maybe a hunter killed the elf and the grim?" Bea asked. It was a thought I'd already had when Marty mentioned it earlier.

I cocked my head to the side. "Yes, it's possible, but if a hunter was responsible, that means they'd basically have gone AWOL."

"What do you mean?"

"Just that hunters aren't supposed to kill indiscriminately—they must have orders to do so."

Bea shrugged. "Maybe they did have orders? Maybe there was a hit on Darragh?"

I took a deep breath. "I don't know… I guess we're going to have to talk to Fox and maybe we can get him to help us with the autopsy." Since Fox and Prince Reynard were one and the same person, I figured I could kill two birds with one stone.

"Why does Reynard go by Fox?" Bea asked.

"Because he's also a detective of sorts and doesn't want to blow his princely cover."

"But everyone knows he's the prince of the Autumn Court, right?"

I shrugged. "I mean… I guess so?"

After dinner, I dropped Bea off at her house and then

went home to wash away the frustrations of the day. A hot shower and a mug of chamomile tea was just what I needed and luckily, Angelo was nowhere to be found.

***

The next morning, I headed to my office, stopping off at Poppy's store along the way to pick up more of my *Repelling Potion*. The guilt I'd recently felt regarding my kiss with Roy was still present and accounted for, but I shoved it to the dark recesses of my mind so I could focus on the task at hand.

When I walked through the door, I found Wanda standing at the counter, talking with Poppy. It was perfect timing—I could use the extra brain power.

After the customary greetings, I filled them both in on everything that had happened over the last day or so.

"Do you think the murders have anything to do with Janara?" Wanda asked, introducing an angle I hadn't thought about before. And, judging from Poppy's expression, she hadn't either.

"I don't know. If they are related, I can't imagine what the connection might be," I replied, shrugging. I wasn't really sure how Janara would have played a part when she and her faerie accomplices were all locked up within a magic faerie circle in the middle of the forest.

"Maybe we should check the circle where Janara and her attendants are being held," Poppy suggested. "Just to make sure they haven't somehow escaped?"

"That's a good idea," I replied.

***

About twenty minutes later, the three of us stood

around a bowl of water as Poppy dropped a few dropperfuls of *Dream Oil,* which was meant to cause a prophetic dream, but could also, apparently, cause waking visions.

"Here, anoint yourselves with this," she said, handing Wanda a blue glass bottle.

"What is it?" Wanda asked.

"*Faerie Spirit Oil,*" Poppy answered. "It's a new one I've started carrying at the store, and you're supposed to use it when working with the fae. I think it might help us more easily conjure the faerie ring."

Wanda nodded and rubbed some of the oil into the pulse points in her neck and her temples. I did the same.

Then we held hands while we closed our eyes and hovered over the bowl of water.

"*Flame of fire, flame of light,*" Wanda said and at the sound of sizzling, I opened my eyes to see a flame that popped out of the center of the bowl of water. As I watched it, it flitted this way and that, the yellow slowly giving way to a bright orange and then a deep red.

"*Bring me now the second sight,*" Wanda continued as I closed my eyes again. "H*elp us to see... the circle holding the Winter faerie.*"

Chapter Seventeen

After Wanda finished her spell, the water within the bowl began to cloud over and all three of us could see our reflections. Then a second later, our images dissipated, to be replaced with hundreds of tall pine trees. As the vision continued to unfold, the pine trees yielded until a clearing between them came into view.

The faerie circle…

I leaned even closer to the bowl of water, checking the circle where Janara and her attendants were being held captive. The cracks in the magic holding them prisoner were obvious—they looked like deep striations in the otherwise bright, glowing red of the circle. There were bound to be even more cracks soon because the magic was, little by little, fading.

"I don't know how much longer the circle is going to hold," Poppy said, apparently having noticed the cracks as well.

"We're going to have to work on that," Wanda frowned. "We can't risk Janara and her misfits getting loose."

"No, we can't," Poppy agreed, her face a mask of

concern.

"Well, one thing's for sure—Janara can't be behind the deaths of Cranough or Darragh," I said. "Because even if the magic is cracking, the circle is still standing."

"Right," Poppy said.

"Back to square one," Wanda added.

I was getting very sick of square one.

***

Fifteen or so minutes later, we said our goodbyes, and I drove to Hallowed Homes, letting myself in and making my way to my office, where I promptly plopped down on the sofa that lined the wall across from my desk. I sat there for a few seconds, just staring off into space as I tried to figure out what I should do next.

When I'd mentioned the fact that Taliyah and Reynard could very possibly come face to face with this case, Poppy had reacted exactly how I'd thought she would—she'd said it was a bad idea for either of them to know who the other was before the time was right. Luckily, Reynard didn't know 'Taliyah' was Olwen's human name and, furthermore, he didn't know what she looked like because they hadn't seen one another since they were children. Not only that, but Reynard still thought Olwen was living in Portland.

"We have to do our best to keep them both in the dark as to their… shared destiny," Poppy had said. "We can't be the ones to interfere."

I wasn't sure why we couldn't be the ones to interfere but didn't ask—when it came to magic and magical prophesies, Poppy was right—it was best not to stick our noses where they didn't belong or, in this case, blow the cover of something that wasn't ours to blow.

Reynard and Taliyah aside, I was frustrated because nothing in this case seemed to be coming together. Darragh and Cranough were dead and we still had no leads. And the only possible coroner we'd found wouldn't help us. To say I was frustrated didn't even start to describe the way I felt.

Why are you even bothering yourself with this? I thought.

It was Taliyah's job to solve crimes, not mine. Still, because I was the one who found Darragh and Cranough, this case felt personal to me. Especially when I still couldn't discount the idea that maybe Hallowed Homes was somehow being targeted. I couldn't risk letting something happen like this again if there was even the slightest chance it was in my power to stop it.

Regardless, defeat had begun to set in since I felt like I was so close to the truth and yet, that truth was still alluding me. It was just too much to think about anymore.

***

After a long day, I was no closer to finding any new information, and I was drained—mentally exhausted and my body needed to feed—not that that was anything new. I decided to head directly home so I could try to sleep off my frustration and hunger. I closed up my office after my last employee left for the night and exited the building, locking the front entrance behind me. I began walking toward the parking lot towards the 4Runner, but was surprised to find Poppy, Marty, and Roy waiting for me beside my SUV. And all of them were smiling?

"Hey, workaholic. Got time to hang out with some

friends?" Poppy teased.

"I don't know, guys," I answered on a sigh as my attention fell on Marty. It was strange, but something suddenly clicked in my head and whatever hope I'd had about something potentially existing between the two of us suddenly switched off. I wasn't sure if it was owing to all the disappointment I'd been suffering lately or what, but whatever hope I'd had for the two of us was now nowhere to be found. "It's been a really long day today," I continued.

"Oh, come on. You still need to eat dinner," Poppy coaxed.

"And who can discount the value of a drink when you've had a long day?" Roy echoed.

"How about tomorrow night?" I asked, sounding hopeful.

"What if I told you we have information you might find interesting?" Poppy added, knowing just what would change my mind.

"You should have led with that!" I answered on a laugh, following them down the driveway that led to a sidewalk which meandered into town. "No offense to Roy, but I'm a little sick of the Half-Moon."

"You and me both," Roy answered with a chuckle.

"Well, rumor has it that a little diner opened up at the end of Main Street, called The Broomstick."

"Already been there," Marty said. "And they serve breakfast all day and their pancakes are spot-on."

"Uh-oh, competition," I answered as I looked up at Roy, but he just smiled back at me.

"Nah, a little competition is good for all involved." I couldn't help but notice that his attention settled on Marty.

***

We shuffled into The Broomstick Diner and took a seat at a booth in a back corner. The ambiance was cute —witch themed with an orange and black color palette. The walls were painted orange, the booths black and the floor was hardwood, also stained black. Witches on brooms hung from the ceiling and the waitresses were dressed in black with pointy hats—each of them had a differently colored ribbon adorning their hats. Kitschy but cute.

Marty ordered the pancake breakfast, Poppy ordered a salad, and Roy ordered a steak while I opted for a glass of wine.

"So?" I asked Poppy. "Spill the beans."

"I got the analysis back on the goop that was Darragh."

I looked at her in surprise. "How did you manage that?"

She dropped her gaze to her fingers, which were clearly fidgeting in her lap. "I happen to have a client who's also a scientist at the University in Wailing Hills," she answered. "And I asked a favor."

Wailing Hills was a largish town maybe thirty minutes or so from Haven Hollow.

"Did you ask this scientist friend to run the sample under the radar?" Roy asked her, to which she immediately nodded.

"She's trustworthy," Poppy answered as she faced me again. "Anyway, Darragh was killed by something called *Spirit Bane*."

"*Spirit Bane*?" I repeated, surprised. "Only a high witch or a very powerful faerie could make that." And the more I thought about it, the less sense it made. "Why would a witch or powerful faerie want to kill Darragh or Cranough?"

"Exactly," Poppy said, nodding. "I don't have an answer for you. But, what I can tell you is *Spirit Bane* is not only difficult to make, but it's also very expensive."

"Do you sell it in your store?" Marty asked.

Poppy shook her head. "It's only sold on the black market and even then, it's really hard to find. Any witch or faerie known to produce it faces serious consequences because the stuff is poison to any supernatural creature. And that means whoever killed Darragh and his attendant was most likely either a witch or a fae."

"Or maybe someone had a witch or faerie purchase it on their behalf," Roy said.

"Yes, that could also be the case," Poppy answered. Then she looked at me. "Have you gotten any further trying to get a coroner to look at Cranough?"

I shook my head and told the story of how Bea and I had come across Burian and learned about his employer, Prince Reynard.

"Why would Fox want a brownie to run autopsies in private?" Roy asked.

I shook my head. "It seemed odd to me too and from the sound of it, part of Burian's oath was only to work for Reynard, er Fox, so whatever Fox has going, he's doing his best to keep it under cover."

"Do you think Fox could have had something to do with the deaths of Darragh and Cranough?" Marty asked. "I mean… is it coincidental that Cranough was also from the Autumn Court?" He paused a moment. "Maybe Cranough was leading some sort of uprising against Reynard and Reynard capped him."

Poppy immediately shook her head. "Fox might be a bit underhanded at times, but he's no murderer."

I couldn't help but notice how she jumped to Fox's defense immediately and, in general, Poppy seemed overly defensive of Fox. Or was I just becoming suspicious of everyone now?

"Have you forgotten you were pretty sure Fox was responsible when Finn went missing?" Roy reminded her.

A crimson flush spread across her cheeks. It was hard to determine if it was sadness or anger as she quickly tried to shift gears to contain her physical reaction. "That was different. Finn's disappearance happened before I really got to know Fox."

"Do you really know Fox well now?" I asked.

She cocked her head to the side. "I would say I know him well enough now that I think he's a good person and I couldn't imagine he'd be behind this case."

"That's what the neighbors say about almost every murderer who happens to live beside them," Marty said.

"I don't know how innocent Fox is," Roy continued. "When he trapped Janara and her retinue in a magic circle, he effectively tossed them into an eternal prison —and one could argue that he did so to ensure his own reign."

"Or he secured a danger that threatened us all," Poppy responded.

Marty faced Poppy again as he exhaled a deep sigh. "It could also be argued that Fox used you to make his life easier, Pops."

I noticed Roy scowled at Marty's term of affection for Poppy.

"How do you figure that?" Poppy demanded, crossing her arms against her chest.

"The point is," Roy nearly interrupted. "None of us knows him very well and from everything I've seen and heard, it sounds like he's pretty self-serving."

"That seems a bit harsh," Poppy continued.

"Harsh or not, I don't think we're wrong here," Roy said.

"Do you really think Fox is capable of murder?" Poppy asked Marty and Roy pointedly.

Marty was the first to shake his head and then paused, with a sigh. "I don't know. I'm not saying he is or isn't, but I don't think we should be so quick to rule him out as a possibility."

"I need some air," Poppy announced in a frustrated tone as she got up from the table and headed toward the front of the diner. She stepped out the entrance doors as the three of us looked at one another with questioning glances. Why was she so hellbent on defending Fox? Were the two of them really *that* close?

"I think we pissed her off," Roy said.

"Yeah, I'm going to go after her and see if I can talk her down," Marty said as he started to stand up.

"I think she needs some alone time," Roy said, putting his hand on Marty's arm to stall him.

"Or she needs someone to let her know we aren't trying to gang up on her," Marty argued, starting to stand up again.

I put a hand on each of them, not wanting this rivalry to erupt into World War III. Besides, there was something else I wanted to talk to her about—the situation regarding Roy and me. I just… it had been eating at me and every time I saw Poppy, the memory of the kiss that had passed between Roy and me wasn't far behind. Maybe if I told her I'd made a mistake and that I only considered Roy a friend—maybe then the guilt about breaking our girl code would go away?

"I'll go check on her," I volunteered, feeling like it

was my fault if Poppy was offended. I mean, I was the one who'd first suggested that Fox might be the bad guy. Maybe it was time to apologize…

Stepping outside the restaurant, I found Poppy sitting on a bench to one side of the doors, dabbing something on her skin. The night breeze caught the scent and wafted it towards me, filling my nostrils with a lovely mixture of sandalwood, citrus, and something I couldn't quite put my finger on. I wasn't sure whether she was anointing herself with a potion or merely refreshing her perfume, but the scent was heavenly, all the same.

"I'm sorry I upset you, Poppy," I offered as I sat down beside her.

She jerked her head up toward me and her expression was one of surprise as she dropped the small vial still in her hand, back into her purse.

"Why are you sorry?" she asked, scooting to one side of the bench to offer me a seat beside her.

I shrugged and sat down, looking up at the almost starless night that enveloped us. The last few nights had been exceptionally dark—the moon had been hidden behind constant cloud cover. Like everything else going on at the moment, I wondered if the pitch darkness was a bad omen. Magic worked in mysterious ways, and during my time in Haven Hollow, I'd learned that situations which might seem completely insignificant could turn out to be ominous in retrospect.

"For a lot of reasons, I guess," I started on a sigh. "I feel like we all ganged up on you back there. And it's my fault you've been dragged into yet another debacle that you shouldn't be involved in."

"What do you mean?"

I shrugged. "Just that it seems like every time

something bad happens in this town, you somehow end up in the middle of it." I took a deep breath, fully aware this wasn't the only subject for which I felt guilty. "It's not fair to you and I've been just as guilty of drawing you into the drama as anyone else."

"You don't have to apologize for any of that, Fifi," Poppy started, giving me that motherly and sweet smile of hers. "I'm happy to be involved because I'm happy to help you as much as I can and I want to get to the bottom of this mystery just as much as you do."

"I appreciate that."

"And you don't have to apologize for what happened earlier. You guys weren't ganging up on me— we just had a difference of opinion and that's what I was just out here reminding myself. We're all welcome to our own thoughts and beliefs and we just happen to disagree where Fox is concerned. But, I'm not offended."

"I'm glad to hear that," I answered, giving her a hollow smile as the heavier truth continued to weigh me down. Yes, I felt guilty about involving Poppy and potentially offending her with my comments about Fox, but I felt even guiltier about a completely unrelated subject.

Feeling Poppy's eyes on me, I continued, lowering my voice to be sure the others didn't hear me in case they happened on us without me noticing. "I'm also sorry... about Roy."

Chapter Eighteen

"Roy?" Poppy replied, glancing in my direction with surprise. "Why would you be sorry about Roy?"

"Um, well…" I started, suddenly unable to find the words. It was like they were stuck in my throat and wouldn't come up, no matter how I encouraged them. "Well, I'm not exactly sure how to put this but… I know you guys just recently broke up and I just… feel guilty because he and I… we've been hanging out a little bit, just platonically," I quickly attached the last words as her expression moved from surprise to something warmer. "I just… didn't want you to get the wrong impression. I mean, I don't want you to think Roy and I are… *together*. Because we're not—we're completely, totally, one-hundred-percent *not* together."

Poppy laughed. "Fifi…"

"And I have zero intention or interest in getting together with him—we're just really good friends and we're going to remain really good friends. I just… didn't want you to think anything was going on behind your back, because I promise it isn't."

"Fifi…"

"I'm still not exactly sure why the two of you broke up, but I'm fully aware of girl code and how it's totally not cool to date a good friend's ex and I would never do it. Besides, Roy told me he's still holding out hope that the two of you might work it out. And I'd be super happy for you both if you did." I wasn't sure I was supposed to mention that last subject, but the words sort of shot out of my mouth before I could stop them. Then I paused long enough to catch my breath as Poppy gave me an encouraging smile.

"Is that everything you wanted to say?" she asked. I just nodded. "Well, I appreciate your concern and I appreciate the girl code, but I want you to know that whatever existed between Roy and me, it's over. And it's going to remain over." She nodded as her eyes settled on something in the distance. I noticed with interest that she didn't seem... upset by what she was saying. It was more like she not only recognized the fact that she and Roy weren't good for each other (at least in her mind) but that she'd also accepted it. "As much as I care about Roy and I imagine I'll always love him in some way, we just aren't right for each other and I'm... I'm alright with that."

"Are you sure?" I asked, feeling a little dejected for Roy because I'd been holding out hope for the two of them. I'd always thought they made a great couple, and he definitely seemed like he wanted to fix things between the two of them.

She nodded. "I'm more than sure. In fact, if you decided you wanted to date Roy, I would encourage you."

"You would?" I asked with a frown, surprised. I just... hadn't expected her to feel this way at all.

"Yes," she answered with another big smile. "I want Roy to be happy and since that happiness can't be with me, I'd love to see him find it with someone else."

I returned her smile and couldn't help but notice just how big her heart was. Poppy was a very special person, and I was so honored to call her my friend.

"And who knows," she continued as she gave me a strange expression. "Maybe he can find that happiness with you?"

I felt my eyes widen as I immediately shook my head because I just couldn't think of Roy that way, even though the succubus begged to differ. "Well, I appreciate that, but given my horrible luck when it comes to dating and men, I'd rather just keep Roy as my friend. I mean... I definitely wouldn't want to risk our friendship by dating him when all of my romantic relationships end up blowing up in my face."

Poppy cocked her head to the side and gave me a knowing expression. "Well, maybe your dating experiences have been less than perfect because you weren't with the right men."

"You think?"

She nodded. "Once you find the right man, I know everything will work out for you."

I liked the sound of that, even if I didn't really believe it... at all. Relationships and me were like oil and water. "I wish that 'right man' would walk into my life sometime soon," I continued on a sigh.

Poppy shrugged. "Who knows, maybe he already has?"

I glanced down at my hands and felt a bit of sadness overtake me. "I don't think so," I answered as I shook my head. Then I looked up at her again, figuring I might as well get the whole truth out. "I actually..." I started to laugh because I was embarrassed by this second part. "I actually had a little crush on Marty."

"On Marty?" she asked, seeming taken aback.

I nodded. "Yeah, but that was before I realized he was in love with you and now I just think of him as a friend."

Poppy shook her head and her expression was one of total shock and, more so, confusion. "What? Marty's not in love with me, silly. We're just… really good friends." I looked at her and frowned, and she gave me an expression of innocence. "I mean it!" she insisted. "Marty's not in love with me." She said the words again as if she were trying to convince herself, just as much as she was trying to convince me.

"Um," I started. "I'm pretty sure he *is* in love with you."

But she insisted on shaking her head—repeatedly. "I'm afraid the rumor mill has gotten that one completely wrong. Marty and I are just friends."

I didn't want to point out that the rumor mill was actually Roy, someone who likely knew what he was talking about, but I wasn't sure what else to say. I was still stunned that she seemed to have no clue about something that was obvious to anyone who paid any attention to the two of them. I mean, I hadn't known it before Roy told me, but that was only because I hadn't been *looking* for it. And now that I'd paid attention when Marty and Poppy were together, his love for her was clear as day. Except, apparently, to Poppy.

"I'm sorry," I started, not wanting to further offend her. I'd already done a good job of that with the whole Fox conversation. "I was under the impression you knew or guessed Marty was interested in you." There was no need to force the issue. If it were true, Poppy would either see it for herself, or Marty would eventually tell her how he felt whenever he was ready.

"Well, now that we've gotten that whole Marty rumor put to bed, let's get back to you and Roy," she said, seemingly uncomfortable with having the magnifying glass turned on her and Marty. She patted my leg and gave me another big smile.

"There is no '*me and Roy'*."

"Well, if at any time, you find yourself interested in taking things to another level with Roy, don't let me stand in the way." She paused and then gave me an expression to show just how serious she was. "I mean it, Fifi."

"Thanks, but…"

Her smiled broadened. "In fact, I think you *should* date Roy—you'd be really cute together. And you have a lot in common."

"We do?" I asked with a frown.

She nodded. "Sure. You both have similar long lifespans. You both want to have normal family lives. And you both want children." Then she paused and looked at me. "Wait… *do* you want children?"

I nodded. "I mean, yeah eventually… if I met the right guy, and we got married and all of that..."

"Right," she said, as if she were still proving a point. "Besides, Roy's a sasquatch, and that means he's one of only a few creatures who could attend to your energy needs without losing too much of himself. I mean, really… it's almost like you two were meant to be!"

Now, I was the one studying her expression in search of answers. Not only was she not opposed to me dating Roy, but she was encouraging it? A part of me was relieved to know she wasn't upset about the two of us hanging out most recently, but a small part of me wondered why she was downright enthusiastic about it.

"It's almost like you *want* me to date Roy."

She was quiet for a few seconds as she pondered my comment. Then she shrugged. "Maybe I do."

"Hmm."

"I love Roy enough to want him to be happy, and we weren't happy with each other—mainly because we weren't... *right* for each other." She inhaled deeply. "And once I realized that much, I had to let him go. I don't think he truly understands that yet, but he will in time." She took another deep breath. "Regardless, he still deserves to be happy and so do you. And you both have an amazing friendship and what better base is there for a relationship?"

I gave her a look. "Couldn't I say the same about you and Marty?"

She immediately shook her head. "No, that's a little different."

"It is?"

She was quiet a moment. "Yes..."

"Why?"

"Well, I'm, um, I'm taking some time off from dating and like I said, Marty's never given me any inclination that he's even interested in me so it's basically a moot point." Then she tapped my knee again as if she were my mother, trying to drive home a point. "But we were talking about you and Roy... and on that subject... whatever decision you make is yours to make," she continued. "But I want it known that I have absolutely no issue with you dating Roy."

"Well, I appreciate that," I started, even as my mind was already made up that Roy and I were just friends and friends we'd remain.

"We should probably get back to our boys before they worry about whatever girl talk we're having," she said with a laugh as she stood up and started for the door of the diner. There was a little pep in her step now that hadn't been there before and I had to wonder if she'd somehow gotten something off her chest at the same time I had?

I watched her walk away and then stood as I sighed loudly into the pitch-black night before walking back toward the entrance to the diner. I opened the door and started to enter, but was stopped by a familiar rank smell that wafted toward me, carried on the breeze down the sidewalk. Closing the door, I turned around to face the street and curled my nose in disgust as a second later, dawning realization overcame me.

It was that same awful smell from the night I'd ventured into Hollow Cemetery when I found the remains of Darragh and Cranough! Yes, it was that same smell of rot and decay and that had to mean that whoever had been present at the graveyard when both had met their ends, was now loitering around The Broomstick diner! I looked around, squinting into the near darkness surrounding the building to see if there was anyone in the darkness, but I couldn't see anyone or anything. For all intents and purposes, I was alone out here.

Now uncomfortable and slightly nervous, I opened the door and stepped inside the diner, my attention immediately drawn to a scene unfolding near the bar area. When I recognized those involved, I groaned as I headed in that direction.

Ramona was cornered against the far wall, situated at one end of the bar, between two adjoining areas. Her adversary's back was facing me, but it only took me a second or two before I recognized his hair, his build, and his clothing. It was Angelo.

Ramona was arguing quietly with him, but his

responses weren't as quiet, though I couldn't make out exactly what he was saying. As to what in the world Angelo could possibly want with Ramona was beyond me—she wasn't exactly his... *type.*

I could see she was on the brink of tears, so I made a beeline for the two of them, intending to position myself between them. When I walked up to them, though, Angelo didn't even notice me—until I stepped in front of him, blocking his access to Ramona.

"What the hell are you doing?" I demanded, glaring at my brother, who glared right back at me.

"Mind your own business, Fifi," he growled, managing to get a grip on Ramona's arm, despite my best efforts to keep him away from her. It was then that Roy and Marty emerged from behind me. Poppy was just behind them, and all three wore expressions of shock and concern.

"What's going on?" Roy thundered in a voice that hinted to the feral sasquatch within him.

"I was just trying to find that out," I answered, keeping my eyes on Angelo, who ignored us as he wrapped his fingers around Ramona's arm, just above her frail wrist, and attempted to pull her out from behind me.

"Let her go right now!" I yelled at my brother as Roy took a step closer. I turned and gave him a look that said I wanted to handle this situation myself. Roy just nodded and took a step back, but made no motion to leave, which was just as well because it felt good knowing he and Marty and Poppy were there for backup. Not that Marty would really be able to hold his own against Angelo, since Marty was just a human...

"You don't know what she's done!" Angelo growled back at me.

Chapter Nineteen

"Whatever it is, I'm sure you deserved it," I answered. "Now back away from her before I'm forced to get Roy involved."

Angelo paused for a moment or two, but then stepped away from Ramona, apparently not wanting to take his chances with an angry sasquatch. At least he still had that much sense.

When Angelo was a safe distance from Ramona, I felt my anger get the better of me. Things with my brother had always been strained, but this was now the last straw. "I'm sick and tired of you," I seethed. "I've already given you multiple warnings, Angelo, and you haven't listened to one of them." He gave me an expression that said he didn't give a damn about me or my warnings. "Anyway, congratulations because you've pushed me to my breaking point."

"What does that mean?"

"It means we're done."

"Done?"

I nodded. "I want you out of my house and you're fired from Hallowed Homes."

His expression then turned from angry to downright hostile. "You wouldn't dare!"

My jaw was tight. "My family duties only extend so far, and you've already used more than your fair share of my goodwill."

"Our parents," he started, but I interrupted, shaking my head.

"They'll understand or they won't understand. Either way, I don't care. All I do care about is the fact that I'm done with you—as my brother and as my employee." I glared at him, unwavering. This moment had been a long time coming, and I felt justified in my decision. Bea was right—I should have done this years ago. "And I don't want to see you ever bullying another of my employees again."

That brought up an interesting subject—just what was Angelo doing with Ramona? Was he trying to intimidate her into quitting? Was she just the first on his list of my employees? I had a strong feeling that's exactly what he was trying to do—ruin me by getting all my employees to quit.

"You have no idea what you're involved in," he snarled as he looked at me. Though his comment was cryptic, I didn't want to push for an explanation. Whatever Angelo had to say, he could keep it to himself because as of this moment, I was finished with him. For good. And if our parents had something to say about that, they could say it.

"I want you and your stuff out of my house by tomorrow morning," I hissed back at him.

His glare deepened. "You are so clueless about what's going on right underneath your nose," he said on an acidic chuckle. "You have no idea how much I'm going to enjoy watching everything go to hell around you."

He gave Ramona a look of raw contempt before smirking at me and walking away. Then he shook his head at Roy, laughed snidely and started sauntering out of the restaurant.

My blood was boiling, not only due to Angelo's bizarre words, but also because I didn't like the fact that he'd manhandled Ramona—someone who was like a toothpick... well, an incredibly frail, six-foot tall toothpick. Ramona was equally as delicate mentally. How dare my brother give her cause for alarm? And why would he?

"Are you okay?" I asked her.

She nodded, but refused to look me in the eyes. Instead, she flagged down the bartender and asked for her check. I looked at Roy and gave him an expression that said everything was okay now. He nodded and led Marty and Poppy back to our table as I turned to face Ramona again.

"Can you... tell me what happened?"

She shrugged. "There isn't really much to tell. I was having a late dinner and Angelo turned up to talk business, or at least that's what I thought he wanted to talk about. But then he just ended up yelling at me and when I'd had enough and attempted to leave, he pinned me against the wall." Her lower lip quivered. "Then you showed up."

Much to my surprise, she burst into tears. Reaching forward, I grabbed a few napkins and handed them to her while she sat back down in her swivel stool and dabbed at her eyes. Wraiths weren't known for being very emotional types and they didn't like being touched in general, so I kept my hands to myself and just tried to comfort her with my presence.

Hopefully she'd get control of herself soon, before any humans nearby took note of the black wetness streaking down her cheeks. Hags, wraiths, and others of that ilk cry black tears that have the consistency of thin motor oil. And because we were in the midst of a human establishment, Ramona had to be careful about anyone seeing her and the blackness coming out of her eyes.

"What was Angelo yelling at you about?" I asked once she seemed to calm down a bit.

She shrugged as she wiped away the last of the black smears on her face. She pulled out a small mirror from her purse and checked her reflection, dabbing at a few small dark specks that remained. I watched as she retrieved a small compact and pressed a bit of makeup into the blotchy spots left behind to cover them up.

"He said he was planning to take over Hallowed Homes when it inevitably went belly up," she started, as my blood boiled with anger to hear her words. "He was planning to buy it from the bank, because he was fairly sure you'd go bankrupt and wouldn't be able to keep it."

"How nice," I managed.

She nodded, as if to say she understood my anger. "Of course, I told him he was delusional, and that I enjoyed working for you and Hallowed Homes."

"I appreciate that," I managed with a smile, but I was still beyond upset with my brother. "What else did he say?"

Ramona shrugged. "After his comment about Hallowed Homes, he changed the subject and started talking about... other things."

"Other things?"

She nodded and looked down at her long and bony fingers. I could tell she was uncomfortable. "Things that were upsetting," she continued. I thought she might start crying again, but when she looked up, her face was dry, just twisted into a mask of disgust.

"What sort of other things?" I almost didn't want to ask, but I had to know. I had to understand just how much my brother wanted to destroy me.

She managed to hold the tears back as she spoke, but she was trembling and her long fingers nervously shredded the remains of a napkin on the bar in front of her.

"He said that when he takes over Hallowed Homes, I wouldn't have a position there unless I performed certain… *favors* for him." If it were possible for a wraith to blush, that's exactly what she did.

I felt my stomach drop and was instantly repulsed. I just didn't understand how Angelo could demand such awful things from Ramona. It was just… wrong on every level. If it were possible for a wraith to blush, that's exactly what she did.

"What sort of favors?" I asked, even though I really didn't want to. But, I had to know because this wasn't like my brother. As terrible as he was and was proving himself to be, I just didn't think in a million years he'd come onto Ramona because she… just didn't look anything like the women he usually got sexually involved with. They were of the bombshell, curvy and gorgeous type and Ramona… well, Ramona looked more like a skeleton—a *librarian* skeleton.

"You know…" she said, looking down at her hands. "*Sexual* favors."

I wasn't sure how I was supposed to even respond, but I couldn't suppress the shock flowing through me. I'd never known Angelo to have anything to do with less than model-perfect women. And it wasn't as though he was down on his female luck—his incubus powers made him irresistible to anyone he set his sights on, so he had little issues in that area. Even when he'd used his powers to sway clients while Ophelia was in charge of Hallowed Realty, he was picky about the women he chose.

Still, Angelo had no shame. I couldn't help but think this was just another game of his, but his reasoning was unclear... until it wasn't. Angelo was hell-bent on taking over Hallowed Homes, as Ramona had mentioned. And that meant he was doing his best to force me out. What better way than to attempt to scare my employees away? In coming onto Ramona, an older and decidedly spinster-like woman, he was trying to make her so uncomfortable that she quit. It wasn't that he actually had any sexual interest in her.

"I'm going to go home now," she announced as she stood. "This has been a most tiring evening."

"Okay, Ramona. And once again, I'm very sorry for whatever my brother said to you."

She nodded and gave me a quick smile, before disappearing out the door. I clenched my teeth as I tried to calm down, but there was little chance of that happening. I just couldn't understand Angelo or his gall. Or his complete hatred for me—because, truly, that's what this had to be. The fact that he was conspiring to take my business away from me and approaching my employees and trying to intimidate them—it showed how little I meant to him. And after I'd opened my house to him, allowed him to live with me while his floors were being installed... Bea and Libby were right—my heart was too big where my brother was concerned and he was making a fool of me.

Well, not any longer. He and I were done for good. It was one thing to undermine me constantly, but to sexually harass and threaten my employees was another.

I took a deep breath to calm myself and walked back to the table where Poppy and Marty were looking back at me with expressions of curiosity on their faces.

"Everything okay?" Marty asked.

I nodded as I noticed the missing fourth. "Where's Roy?"

Poppy gave me a quick but slightly nervous smile. "He left. Said he had to get up early tomorrow."

"Oh," I answered.

Rather than interrupt whatever conversation Poppy and Marty were having, and really not wanting to feel like the third wheel, I made my excuses and walked back to Hallowed Homes, where I'd left the 4Runner. It was then that my phone beeped with an incoming text. When I glanced down at it, I realized it was from Roy. It read: *"Hey, I didn't want to hang out with Marty making cow eyes at Poppy all night, so I took off. If you need a place to crash tonight, just come by. I'll make up the couch and sleep there again. You can have my room."*

I thought about going home and having to watch Angelo pack up all his stuff. And then I thought about having to see Angelo at all and decided I'd take Roy up on his offer.

So, jumping into my SUV, I fired up the engine and headed for Roy's. All the way there, I thought about my estranged relationship with my brother and sorely wished things could have been different between us. For as long as I could remember, going back to when I was a little girl, all I'd ever wanted was a big brother who loved me and took care of me—a big brother who protected me. And all I'd gotten was... Angelo.

Well, no brother was better than having *him* as a brother, and from this point forward, I vowed to myself that I would cut all ties with him.

When I reached Roy's house, I put the 4Runner in park and killed the engine and then I just sat there for a few seconds, trying to motivate myself to get out and walk up the steps and knock on the door and inevitably explain everything that had just happened.

I could already feel the weight of the world on my shoulders, but eventually I managed to get out of the 4Runner and then I trudged across the driveway and started up the stairs. I didn't even get the chance to knock on the door before Roy pulled it open. Upon seeing him, and his concerned expression, something inside me broke, and I erupted into a fit of tears right there on his front steps.

"Come on," he said as he took a step forward and pulled me into his arms and I sobbed and probably snotted all over his t-shirt.

He walked me inside, shut the door behind us, and led me to the couch, which was enjoying the heat from an enormous fire in the hearth. He sat me down and then kneeled in front of me as I continued to bawl and feel sorry for myself.

"It's okay, Fifi, everything is going to be okay," he said as he reached up and pushed a stray tendril of my hair behind my ear.

"How can you say that?" I asked, shaking my head as I tried to wipe away my tears with my arm. "When you don't know that everything is going to be okay? As of right now, everything is going to shit."

"What happened?"

So I told him about the conversation with Ramona and every awful detail she'd told me. He reached behind himself and produced a glass of red wine he must have been drinking before I arrived. Handing it to me, he gave me a big grin.

"I think you need this more than I do."

I nodded, because he was right. And in the next minute, I downed the whole thing.

"Fifi, believe me when I tell you that I think Angelo is the biggest asshole Haven Hollow has ever seen," Roy started as he reached for the empty glass and placed it back on the coffee table. Then he took both of my hands in his. I wasn't sure if he was offering me to feed from him, but my body immediately reacted by doing just that.

"But," I started.

"But it doesn't seem… *right* that he would have tried to seduce Ramona." He shook his head. "I've seen the quality of woman Angelo bothers with and Ramona… isn't it."

I nodded. "I don't think he had any plans of… going through with… *it*," I managed, feeling uncomfortable talking about sex with Roy. We just… we were friends and conversations like this seemed off-limits somehow.

"Then?"

"I think he was just trying to make her so uncomfortable that she'd quit working for me. And I believe she was only the first on his list of my employees to bully."

Roy nodded. "That makes more sense."

He stood up and started for the kitchen, the hardwood floors beneath him squeaking with his sizable weight. I couldn't help my gaze as I took him in from head to toe, noticing how his broad shoulders tapered into a narrowish waist and then ended in legs that seemed to go for miles. He was wearing his boxers and a t-shirt and I could clearly see his thigh muscles as he walked. Not to mention the muscles in his back and arms that seemed intent on driving me to distraction.

"You want another glass?" he asked as he lifted the bottle of wine and smiled at me.

I just nodded and watched him grab a second glass as he walked both it and the bottle back to the couch. He sat down beside me and started refilling my glass, as well as his own. Then he handed one of them to me.

"Cheers to your life settling down and all this crap fading away," he offered.

"Cheers," I answered as I gave him a smile and suddenly felt beyond grateful for his friendship.

He took a few sips of his wine, then set it down on the coffee table, and pulled me into the crook of his body as he wrapped his arms around me. He was so warm, and he felt so good and I could feel the succubus within me pulling his energy, but he didn't seem to mind. Maybe he hadn't said as much, but I could still tell. It was all I could do to keep control of the demoness within me and keep my carnal needs subdued.

***

I awoke to find myself lying on the couch, still in Roy's arms. I couldn't tell what time it was, but it was still dark outside and Roy was snoring lightly. The fire had long since died and the bottle of wine was empty. Feeling a chill, I reached down to the blanket he'd placed on the couch since he'd planned on sleeping here alone, and pulled it over both of us.

Roy shifted, and his snoring stopped. "You want to go sleep in my bed?" he asked.

"No, I want to sleep right here if that's okay," I whispered back.

He didn't respond, other than to wrap his arms firmly around me as I lowered my head back to his chest. After another minute or so, he started gently snoring again.

And it was then that I remembered something—something I'd decided during the night, before I'd drifted off to sleep.

I'd made up my mind.

I'd made up my mind to let it all go.

All of it.

Everything.

Taliyah could handle the murders just like she was supposed to, Angelo could go back home, either to his house or to our parents in New York and I'd focus on making Hallowed Homes so strong that nothing could tear it down.

Not my brother, not my murdered client, nothing.

Chapter Twenty

A week passed, and things were finally beginning to look up. I'd managed to make a sizable sale of a lake house to three sister mermaids, which was a huge relief. Plus, I had other exotic clients lining up to look at some of our properties that were perfect for their specific needs. The plot at Haven Cemetery was still for sale and so far, I hadn't had one lead, but I tried not to let it get me down.

I couldn't help but feel like my newly found good luck was teetering on the edge of a cliff, though, because it was just a matter of time before news of the murders spread to neighboring areas. As far as Haven Hollow was concerned, it now seemed like everyone and their mother was aware of what had happened to Darragh and Cranough. Not surprisingly, all Hallowed Homes recent sales were to outsiders. But, yes, it was just a matter of time before the news spread of a murderer in Haven Hollow who was, as of yet, still roaming free.

All I could do was keep doing what I did best— selling homes. My dedication to the business was already beginning to pay off—my employees had absolutely celebrated my decision to let Angelo go, and they'd been even more thrilled when I distributed his clients and leads between them.

As to Angelo, he'd moved out of my house as promised and I hadn't seen him since the altercation with Ramona a week or so ago.

Ramona appeared to be in much better spirits with Angelo gone—really, it was like she was a totally different person. Tonight, she had an appointment she seemed ecstatic about. She'd been flitting through the office all day in an unusually good mood as she prepared to show what was once a golf course to a family of gnomes who were interested in turning it into a gated community. She'd already given the gnomes a tour of the property a few times and tonight was supposed to be the night they signed on the dotted line.

As to the murders, Taliyah was doing her best, but without anyone to do a proper autopsy on Cranough, she was stuck spinning her wheels. Apparently Taliyah had been trying to reach Fox Aspen, but he hadn't answered, nor returned any of her calls. When Poppy got involved, he didn't answer her calls either. It could have been that he was ignoring us, or he might have been incredibly busy being Prince Reynard. Either way, he wasn't helping the situation.

And that was part of the reason why I decided to get involved again. I had to try again to get Burian to help us. If Burian could confirm the cause of Cranough's death, that would at least give us more information than we currently had, and maybe it would make the difference between an unsolved case and a soon-to-be solved one.

Leaving the office with renewed determination, I decided not to rely on just myself. Instead, I figured a sasquatch might just be intimidating enough to make Burian talk. So, I made my way to the Half-Moon to ask Roy to accompany me. Once I explained my mission, he was fairly easily swayed.

Within the hour, we were on our way to Cherry Woods.

"I don't know why you think he'll help this time when he wouldn't before," Roy said, looking at me as I drove down the deserted road that led to Burian's building.

"I figured there's nothing quite as intimidating as a sasquatch," I answered with a smile.

"Not sure I'm more intimidating than a demoness," he responded. I just gave him a little smile because I didn't like the title. I didn't think of myself as a *demoness,* even though that was exactly what I was. Regardless, I just thought of myself as Fifi, the girl with too many man problems.

"When was the last time you transformed fully?" Roy asked, as he looked over at me.

"Transformed?" I repeated, but I knew what he was talking about. It was just a subject I hadn't thought about in a long time—mostly because I didn't want to.

"Sure. Into your demoness form."

I swallowed hard. "It's been a while… at least five years, not since…"

"Ah," he answered, clearly not needing me to finish the statement—he knew I hadn't had sex in five years. He gave me an understanding smile, and I just blushed.

"Do you miss being in your full power?"

"Not really," I answered, before I realized saying as much wasn't the full truth. "I mean, I miss feeling completely energized and full of life. Instead, I always have this sort of haze in my mind and I usually feel like

I'm operating at half capacity, you know." I cleared my throat, finding this whole subject uncomfortable. "Of course, it gets a little better after I've fed."

He nodded. "But when you feed now, you aren't really feeding fully."

"Right."

He was quiet for a few seconds and I couldn't help but wonder at the thoughts going through his head. "So if you actually had sex, you'd feel better than you have in the last five years?"

"Probably."

"So…"

I cleared my throat and shook my head. "It's not that simple."

"Not as simple as just having sex?"

I shook my head again, wishing we weren't ten minutes from Burian's because I really didn't want to continue having this conversation. "No."

"Why?"

"Because… um, because if I had sex with someone now, after being… basically abstinent for the last five years, I could do that person serious bodily harm, or even kill him."

"If he were human."

"Right. But, also potentially… if he were some other species too."

He shrugged. "You couldn't kill or hurt me."

I started blushing even more and stared at the road straight ahead, even as I could feel his eyes on me. Why would he say such a thing when we both were completely aware that we only wanted to be friends? "Um, I probably couldn't hurt you."

"Hmm."

Hmm, was right.

"What if…" he started, but I interrupted because I didn't want to know what he was going to ask next. This conversation was already causing me to break out into a cold sweat.

"We really don't have to talk about this, Roy, especially when my focus needs to be on Burian and whether or not he's going to help us."

Roy nodded. "He'll help us."

"How can you be so sure?"

"I'm a sasquatch, remember?" I laughed as he turned to face me again. "Going back to this sex thing." I groaned, and he chuckled. "Fifi, I know you don't want to discuss this, but I think it's important."

I breathed in deeply and then sighed. "I don't know why you think it's important because none of it matters anyway."

"It does matter," he argued. "It absolutely matters."

"Why?"

"Because… well," it was his turn to clear his throat and appear slightly uncomfortable. "What if… what if I offered my body to you sexually?"

I was quiet for a few seconds as a feeling of offensive indignation welled up within me at his choice of words. *Offered his body to me sexually?* He made it sound like he was offering up his corpse for the sake of science.

"Um," I started, not really sure how to respond, but I didn't think anger was a good outlet. I knew Roy and he hadn't tried to offend me—in his mind, he thought he was just helping.

"I don't like the fact that you haven't fed in so long that it's affecting your energy levels," he continued. "And I also don't like it that you're trying to suppress your own identity."

Yes, I could have gotten irritated with him because he was putting his nose into my business—somewhere it definitely didn't belong, but this was just Roy being overprotective Roy. It's just how he was and how he'd always been. "I don't... really think of myself as a succubus."

"But you *are* a succubus and trying to pretend you're anything but isn't doing you any favors."

"I seem to be getting along okay."

"Fifi, you passed out at the last council meeting, you look weaker every time I see you, not to mention that whenever I touch you, your instinct is to immediately absorb my energy... you're body is starving, whether you want to admit it or not."

"Um," I started, but couldn't think of anything more to say.

"If you and I had sex," he continued, as I withered a little more on the inside. Could this conversation be any more clinical and unemotional? I didn't think it could. "I'd be able to withstand whatever came over you. You wouldn't be able to injure or kill me."

"I get that, but I just..."

"And I understand you'd need to feed repeatedly, so it wouldn't be a one-time thing. I'd be fine with that too." Then he nodded as if to prove his point. He didn't say anything more, but just sat there, awaiting my response.

And my response was one of surprise—I was surprised he didn't know me well enough to know that such an agreement would never fly with me. Not when I was as romantic as I was.

"What if you got into a relationship?" I asked, keeping my eyes on the road as I tried to talk myself out of being annoyed with him. He was just trying to help in his insensitive, Roy sort of way. He didn't mean anything by it. He was, as usual, just trying to help.

"Well, then that would put a stop to things but, at this point, I'm not interested in dating anytime soon." He took a breath. "And, of course, if *you* got into a relationship, I'd understand that things would need to stop on your end, as well."

My cheeks felt like they were on fire with embarrassment and humiliation. This conversation was just so... so clinical, so scientific, so completely unemotional. "Well, I appreciate the offer, Roy," I started. "But, I... I'm actually... ahem, I'm saving myself."

"Saving yourself?" he sounded both surprised and confused.

I nodded. "I don't... want to have sex again until I'm in love, or failing that, I want to at least be in a serious relationship. I just... after the last time I had sex, and the guy dumped me the next day, I promised myself I'd do things differently. I promised myself I'd protect... my heart."

Roy's jaw was suddenly tight, and I was worried he was annoyed I was turning him down, that is, until he spoke. "I'm sorry that happened to you—that someone was callous enough to do that to you." He looked over at me. "You didn't deserve to be treated like that."

I nodded. "I know."

"It's that stupid man who's missing out, Fifi, not you."

I gave him a quick smile to let him know I wasn't troubled by what had happened. "It's okay. I learned from it and I know what I want now."

"Well, I commend you for the path you're taking— even if it might not be in the best interests of your succubus. I do think it's in the best interests of Fifi, though."

"Thank you," I answered, and meant it.

"You're a good woman," he continued, the pitch of his voice softening and he refused to take his eyes away from me. "And I'm sure you'll make a man very happy someday and that man will make you equally happy."

I nodded. "That's my hope, anyway."

We both were quiet for another minute or so, before he broke the silence by asking, "What were you and Poppy talking about back at the diner? Before that whole thing with Ramona and Angelo happened?"

I took a deep breath and exhaled before relaying the conversation to him, including Poppy's surprise regarding Marty being in love with her and then her insistence that it wasn't true.

"She's delirious if she thinks he's not in love with her," Roy muttered, shaking his head.

I nodded. "It's pretty obvious to me too, but maybe she's just not comfortable with the idea."

Roy shook his head. "She seemed pretty comfortable with it that night."

I quickly looked over at him. "Is that why you left early?"

He inhaled deeply and the truth was there in his expression, weighing down his eyes. "Yeah, sometimes it just gets… *hard* to be around her and to remember what we had and how we don't have it anymore. Sometimes I just… I'm not sure how to even act around her, you know?"

I nodded, even though I wasn't really sure how that would feel. Usually when one of my relationships ended, I never saw the guy again. And that was probably just as well—I couldn't imagine having to see an ex around town all the time, especially if another person were trying to move in on that ex.

"She sounded like she was pretty much over me, didn't she?" he asked, his gaze riveted to something outside the window.

I wasn't sure what to say on that point. I could lie and say no, but then Roy would just hold onto hope that wasn't really there. But, if I told him the truth, that truth would no doubt hurt him. Yet, maybe the truth would also help him get over Poppy faster? Regardless, honesty was always the best policy.

"Um, I think... I think she's dealt with the relationship and she's been able to... put it behind her, yes."

He nodded. "I can tell."

"I'm sorry..." I started, not really sure what more to say.

"No," he insisted. "I actually... I actually feel better knowing that, I think. No..." He took a deep breath then nodded. "Yeah... I feel better." He looked over at me then and gave me a quick smile. "It's good to know what I already suspected."

"What you already suspected?"

He nodded again. "Poppy and I have no future together. I'd really kind of already realized it, even if I hadn't fully accepted it, but it's always good to know for sure."

"I can understand that. Maybe it makes it easier to move on?"

"Maybe."

I felt like he needed a little pep talk—something to help him get out of whatever sadness he might have been feeling about Poppy and their failed relationship. "You will find the right woman for you too, Roy," I offered, giving him a quick smile before returning my eyes to the road. "And when you do, she won't let go of you for anything."

"That sounds nice."

"When it happens for you, it won't happen to someone more deserving." I turned to face him as we pulled up in front of Burian's building. Once I put the 4Runner in park, I reached over and touched his hand before he opened the door. He looked at me in surprise.

"Since I've come to Haven Hollow, you are one of very few men who treated me like I was actually more than just my face and body."

"You are so much more than just your beauty, Fifi."

I smiled at him, but wanted to get the rest of my thoughts out because... I felt like he needed to understand just what a great man he was. And that even if things with Poppy hadn't worked out, that didn't reflect poorly on him. "All my life, because of what I am, men have pawed at me, and pretty much made me feel like an object," I continued, my voice cracking a little as I fought back emotions I wasn't aware were lying beneath the surface. "When I was working for you, it was the closest to normal I've ever felt. You didn't treat me like every other man has. You didn't let other men treat me badly either."

"Because I care about you."

I nodded, because I knew he cared about me. He always had. "You listened to me, too. You were always there to lend an ear and give a kind word when I needed one. I can't remember you ever judging me or trying to tell me what I should think or feel or do or say. You were just there for me to talk to, and I appreciated that. I still do."

"And I'm always here for you, Feef. I always will be."

"Thank you."

I released his hand and watched as he undid his seatbelt and then opening the passenger door, stepped onto the curb. I followed suit and as I turned to face the building, at first, I was a bit concerned to find that the boards across the window had been reattached. How were we going to get in now? I'd planned on climbing through like Bea had last time and then opening the back door from the inside for Roy, who was far too large to fit through the narrow opening created by the missing boards, but now neither of us could get in.

"Crap. We're going to have to pull those boards off," I said.

"I don't think so," Roy replied, heading toward the front doors on the opposite end to where Burian had broken in. When we approached them, I noticed they looked like they were older than the two of us put together. I tried to get a glimpse around Roy to see what he had in mind, but that was a tall order.

Chapter Twenty-one

Much to my surprise, Roy merely grabbed the iron door handles, and pulling against the ancient things, he simply broke the double doors off their hinges. Yes, bringing Roy had been a good idea.

Luckily, the front doors were located on the exact opposite end to where Bea and I had first come across Burian, so I could only hope the noise hadn't traveled all the way to the other end of the building.

We slipped through the busted doors and started for the far end of the hall, where Burian's office was located. We tiptoed all the way there, making little to no sound at all, and once we arrived at the end of the hall, I was able to detect the outline of a small creature standing in the center of the room—Burian.

Unlike the last time I was here with Bea, the room was better lit, at least in the area of the exam table. Still, it cast shadows around the room, allowing us to remain hidden while Burian stood focusing on his work. As far as I could tell, he hadn't been alerted to the fact that Roy had barreled through the front doors as easy as you please.

We remained still and watched as Burian bent over (standing atop a five-step stool) and tended to a body laid out on a slab, performing an autopsy as far as I could tell. The more I focused on the creature atop the table, the more I realized she was a faerie, and based on her choice of clothing (a tan shirt and a dark green skirt which were currently heaped in a pile beside her body), she was from the Autumn Court. I couldn't make out her features from this distance, but I could make out the dark red curls of her hair.

As my eyes focused in on the darkness, I strained to make out the corners of the basement and that was when I realized we weren't alone with Burian. I nudged Roy to look in the direction of the alcove off to one side of the room. In front of the wall of cabinets stood a dark figure, watching Burian intently. I wondered if Burian knew he had three guests observing him and was simply ignoring all of us, or if he was just oblivious to our presence at all.

We didn't have to remain curious for long as the other onlooker spoke up, taking a step out of the shadows and towards the light, revealing himself to be Fox Aspen.

"Do you know the cause of death yet?" he asked.

Burian didn't look up from his work. "Nae so far."

"Why not?" Fox sounded like he was out of patience.

Burian shrugged. "There don't appear to be nothing wrong with the body so far."

"Except for the fact that it's dead, you mean."

"Aye. Yet, there be no visible wounds."

"What shall you do next then?"

"Me run some tox screens to see what they turn up."

"Very good," Fox breathed out on a sigh. "I'm

mostly interested to know if a Winter agent snuck into our court. I know they're frantically trying to locate the queen regent and I can't allow them to trace Janara and her retinue to the Hollow."

"Aye."

"You must work faster, Burian, time is of the essence."

"Me going as fast as me can."

"Well, it's not fast enough!" Fox yelled, making my heart skip a beat, as he threw his hands into the air. "The magical protections sealing Janara in the circle are already cracking! One good hit from a powerful vassal of the Winter Court will shatter them permanently and set Janara free!"

Roy and I exchanged a look. So, what Poppy and Wanda had revealed with their scrying was true. Just like I'd witnessed, the magic keeping Janara and company prisoner was cracking, threatening to put Haven Hollow in danger.

I looked back at the body on the slab and the more I studied the woman's face, the more I realized I recognized her. She was a faerie I'd recently interviewed for a sales position, named Saffron. I'd planned to call her back and offer her the job, but now that was clearly no longer an option.

What a horrible shame.

The last time I'd seen Saffron, she was all smiles, chatting happily with Ramona and Libby before giving me a huge smile and saying she'd love to join the Hallowed Homes family. And now? Now she was laid out on a table, dead and as cold as the metal below her.

This, then, was another death associated with Hallowed Homes. And that was a truth I had a difficult time facing. It meant Darragh, Cranough and now

Saffron were all related—they were all tied to me and my business.

I swallowed hard as I leaned in to get a closer look and accidentally nudged a small pan to the left of my foot. It scratched across the floor, alerting both Fox and Burian to our presence. I froze, waiting to see what both would do.

Fox just looked vaguely annoyed as he stepped further out of the shadows and turned toward us.

"What are you two doing here?" he demanded.

"We're trying to solve a murder," I answered, my jaw just as tight as his.

"Well, what a coincidence!" he answered with an acidic laugh. "So am I."

"I believe we may be looking for the same person," I continued, starting to come to the conclusion that whoever was murdering people in Haven Hollow, was definitely trying to send Hallowed Homes a message. Or maybe that person wasn't trying to send Hallowed Homes a message so much as he or she was trying to send *me* a message. The more I thought about who that person could be, the more I arrived at only one candidate: *my brother*. It was a realization I didn't want to face, but I couldn't release it from my mind either.

If this was Angelo, Fifi, you have to face it, I told myself. *And he can't get away with it.*

"Why would we be looking for the same person, hmm?" Fox asked, appearing genuinely confused by my statement.

"I found a grim and his elf attendant dead at a graveyard in the Hollow where they were supposed to meet me to view a property I was selling."

"Then neither died of natural causes?" Fox considered, sounding bored.

"Natural causes?" Roy answered with a laugh. "What natural causes do you know of that would kill two separate species at the same place, at the same time?"

Fox cocked his head to the side and then nodded. "A fair point." Then he faced me again. "And this brings you here why?"

"Because I haven't been able to get anyone to do an autopsy. Well, on the elf, anyway. The grim was… um, *dissolved*."

"Yes, as I understand it, grims have the unfortunate tendency to become quite messy when in the clutches of death," Fox answered.

I nodded. "We were able to test the grim's remains, and the test confirmed the presence of *Spirit Bane*, but we can't confirm whether the *Spirit Bane* might also have killed the elf."

"And this elf of which you speak," Fox started.

"Was named Cranough," I answered, waiting to see if the name sparked any interest from Fox. It didn't. "He was a member of the Autumn Court, your court."

Fox inhaled deeply. "Was he?"

"Yes."

"I see." He remained quiet for a few more seconds as I wondered at the thoughts going through his head. As usual, he wore a poker face. "And that brings you here why?" he asked .

"Isn't that fairly obvious?" Roy asked but I reached out and touched his hand in an attempt to warn him not to rile Fox. We needed the elusive fae on our side.

"We came to see Burian, hoping he'd change his mind about helping us," I answered.

"Ah, then you paid Burian a visit earlier, did you?" Fox continued as he gave Burian a frown which caused me to believe Burian had never mentioned Bea's and my visit.

"We did."

"Very good, very good," Fox continued. "And where are the remains of this elf from my court now?"

I shook my head. "I'm not sure. Ta...er the Chief of Police of Haven Hollow had Cranough's body removed from the scene and stored until we could find someone to do an autopsy."

"Then the humans are involved?" Fox asked, clearly irritated.

"No. The Chief of Police isn't... *human*," I answered, not wanting to admit much more than that.

"From what I could recall, your head of police was a man named Cain?" Fox asked as I swallowed hard. "And he was hopelessly human."

"Right, but he... wasn't available to remain the Chief of Police so... someone else took his place," I answered, really not wanting to get into the fact that Fox's princess-intended was now the head of the human police department of Haven Hollow.

"I see," Fox answered. "Back to the remains..."

"Right. So, the Chief of Police had the elf stored. The grim's remains..."

"Are just a slick of ectoplasm," Roy supplied. "But we still have some samples if someone wanted to test it further."

"Then I suppose I shall have to pay this Chief of Police of yours a visit, shan't I?"

"Um, I don't know that that's a good idea," I started, immediately disliking the idea of Taliyah and Fox coming face to face, even as I realized it was probably unavoidable at this point.

"And why should that not be a good idea?"

"Well," I started as Roy gave me a quizzical look—

clearly he hadn't put together the fact that Fox and Taliyah were promised to each other. Actually, I wasn't even sure if Roy knew as much. I cleared my throat. "She doesn't... like outsiders getting involved in Haven Hollow business," I continued, coming up with whatever I could, off the top of my head. Fox frowned at me.

Then I remembered how Fox had refused to return any of our calls. It was a good change of subject. "Where have you been, anyway?" I demanded, throwing my hands on my hips. "Poppy and I have been trying to get in touch with you, but you haven't answered any of our calls, and you haven't returned them either."

"Oh. Sorry about that," Fox answered with a flick of his wrist, which made it seem as though the question wasn't a pertinent one. "I recently hired a new assistant and to say she is incompetent is an understatement."

"What does that have to do with," I started, but he interrupted.

"I had to fire her in the middle of a meeting, and in a fit, she snatched my phone, threw it at me and it shattered against the block wall behind me." Then he shrugged, inspecting his nails with what appeared to be ennui. "I suppose I should be grateful her aim was just as horrid as her office skills." He paused to sigh. "At any rate, I haven't had time to retrieve a replacement phone." Then he paused again as a large smile lit his face. Fox was definitely handsome but I didn't trust him as far as I could throw him. "If you know anyone more qualified, do let me know."

I wasn't sure what to make of his story about his assistant and the phone. I had a good idea it was just a load of BS and the truth was more along the lines of Fox just not wanting to deal with any of us, but there was no way to prove as much and, furthermore, it really didn't matter.

"Ye said there was nae marks on the victims in the graveyard," Burian said, reminding me he was still there.

"Right," I answered.

Fox nodded. "It's the same with Saffron here—her body is completely unblemished."

Burian nodded and then waved toward the body on his table, inviting us to take a closer look. Of course, I already knew her identity, but I decided to keep that information to myself. I just... didn't want Fox to think I had anything to do with any of the deaths and at this stage, I was more interested in what he could tell me about the murders than what I could tell him. Roy had told me once that it was always better to play your cards close to your chest and this was one instance where that advice could serve me well.

"How will you determine what happened to Saffron if there's no evidence of a wound?" Roy asked.

"Well, before ye appeared, me was checking her internal organs," Burian answered.

"Sometimes, you can get a good idea of what happened to a body by examining things like defects or ruptures in organs," Fox supplied.

"And?" I asked.

Burian shook his head. "Nothing of interest so far."

"What about poison?" Roy asked.

Burian nodded as if he were about to get to that point, but Fox beat him to it. I had to half wonder if Fox just liked listening to himself speak. "If there's nothing evident at the bodily level, then Burian shall run tests that might reveal toxins or elevated levels of chemicals that occur naturally or unnaturally in the body."

"Did you find out anything at the bodily level?" I asked.

"Aye, organ failure," Burian answered.

"Saffron's heart gave out, but so far, Burian can't find any defects in her heart or anything that would have affected it so adversely," Fox said. "No clogged arteries, no valve damage, no deficiencies. It's as though her heart just stopped working for no apparent reason."

Burian nodded. "Aye, otherwise, Saffron was in good health."

"Right up to the moment she suffered a fatal heart attack," Fox finished.

"Would *Spirit Bane* cause such a reaction?" I asked.

"Aye," Burian replied.

"Did you test her for *Spirit Bane*?" Fox asked Burian pointedly.

"Nae yet," Burian answered.

"Then test her, man!" Fox nearly yelled.

"Is there anything else that could have caused her heart to fail, besides *Spirit Bane*? Other than just natural causes?" I asked, wanting to calm Fox down.

Burian nodded. "Aye—a demonic or parasitic monster would be me best guess."

"A demonic or parasitic monster?" I repeated, sounding shocked because I was.

Fox nodded. "Such a creature could have caused cardiac arrest by draining the life from poor Saffron or simply frightening her to death."

Meanwhile, Burian took a sample of Saffron's blood and then started down his footstool as he approached a table with a microscope and some other scientific tools of the trade. He placed the blood on a slide and then placed it under the microscope, before studying it.

"Well?" Fox asked.

"What sort of monsters would be able to scare someone to death?" Roy asked.

"Nae, there ain't no *Spirit Bane* in her blood," Burian answered.

Fox, meanwhile, shrugged as he looked at Roy. "A variety of types could literally scare someone to death— a wendigo, a night hag, a wraith, incubi, succubae..." His eyes darted toward me with suspicion as he listed off the last two species, but I couldn't say I was that concerned. Instead, my thoughts were centered around his last sentence.

A wendigo, a night hag...

A wraith.

And then it all suddenly made sense, like a flood of truth opening my eyes to something I hadn't considered before.

The smell of rot coming from the graveyard—it was the same odor I'd detected outside The Broomstick Diner before I'd found Angelo cornering Ramona—it was the scent of death, the scent of the *wraith*.

And that wasn't all. Suddenly, I was reminded of the surprise I'd felt when Ramona had opted to remain at Hallowed Homes when she'd been close to Ophelia...

Ramona had been close to Ophelia...

Then it wasn't Angelo who was behind the murders at all. It was Ramona.

I turned and began hurrying for the exit as I realized the longer I stayed here, the more chance there was of someone else from Hallowed Homes ending up hurt or dead—something I wouldn't allow to happen.

I could hear Roy and Fox's footsteps behind me as they followed in hot pursuit, yelling at me to stop. But, I couldn't stop and there was no time to explain. Yes, I was more than aware that it probably looked like I was guilty because I was running away, but I didn't care. All I could think about was the likelihood of one of my employees going up against Ramona—it was a fight they wouldn't win.

Once reaching the 4Runner, I jumped into it and then looked over at Roy as he appeared in the doorway. "Where are you going?" he yelled. He was big and strong as a yeti, but somewhat slowed by his size.

"I've got to get back to Haven Hollow now!" I insisted, my eyes going wide as the truth rained down on me and I cranked on the engine. "I know who killed Darragh, Cranough and Saffron!"

"Fifi," Roy started, but I put the 4Runner in drive and pulled out of the parking spot.

"I'm sorry, Roy, but I have to take care of this myself," I said, not wanting to put his life at risk because I knew how dangerous this situation was. Furthermore, this was my fight, not his.

I gunned the engine and left the two of them watching me with perplexed expressions.

I had to get back to Haven Hollow as soon as possible. This situation was now literally a matter of life and death and I could only hope the black Sharpie pen I usually carried with me was still there.

Chapter Twenty-two

"We have to go now," I said as I practically dragged Taliyah from her office chair. "We don't have a lot of time."

"What are you talking about?"

"I'll explain on the way," I answered and luckily she agreed to follow me. I led the way to my 4Runner which was parked just out front of the police precinct, but, apparently, that was where she drew the line.

"We're taking my squad car," she insisted.

I didn't argue, but turned around and followed her to the marked police vehicle, jumping into the passenger seat and buckling up as I faced her. "Do you know where the old golf course at the eastern end of Haven Hollow is?"

She nodded. "That's where we're going?"

"That's where we're going. And drive as fast as you can."

"Roger that."

Taliyah didn't mess around. She floored it the whole way and put the sirens on to make sure everyone cleared out of our path. And they did. Along the way, I explained my best guess regarding what was going on.

Prior to arriving at Taliyah's, I'd called Bea to ask if Ramona was still at her meeting with the gnomes at the golf course and Bea had confirmed that she was, something which filled me with dread. I was scared for the safety of the gnomes (since Ramona was the one who was trying to ruin Hallowed Homes, probably out of loyalty to Ophelia, I believed the gnomes were now in danger). Ramona had already killed my first exotic client, and I could only imagine the gnomes were next on her list.

Maybe ten minutes after leaving the police station, we arrived at the golf course. "This way," I called to Taliyah as she climbed out of the driver's seat and I led the way.

The would-be gnome community was located behind a two-story industrial looking building which had served as the offices of the golf course personnel at one point. In order to access the golf course, you had to enter the building. The gnomes were planning on keeping the building to use it as a security gate of sorts. The building was accessed by key code and because Hallowed Homes had sold this property to the gnomes, I had the key code. I could only hope it still worked.

Walking up to the door, I yanked my phone out from my purse, looked up the code and entered it. To my undying relief, the door beeped twice and then I pulled it open. Bolting through the door, I was stopped dead in my tracks by an odd sight. Angelo was standing in the middle of the lobby, maybe fifty feet away, with what looked like a couple dozen gnomes cowering behind him. Approaching from the other side of them Ramona, her back to us.

"Step away from the little bastards and I might let

you live," she snarled at my brother and it took me a second to put together the fact that this was the same Ramona I'd been working with for years. I'd just never heard this level of... confidence in her tone. Nor anger.

"They've done nothing to you, Ramona," Angelo spat back. "If you have a problem with me or my sister, then you can take it up with us directly. Leave them out of it."

I was equally floored to find my brother standing up for the gnomes—in general, he wasn't the type to do anything heroic or altruistic. In fact, this was the first time I'd ever witnessed him acting out of selflessness.

I waited, remaining in the shadows of the entryway, just beyond the door, in order to listen. Taliyah was behind me, trying to push past my extended arm, but I shook my head at her and continued to hold her back. She was no match for Ramona anyway, and I wanted to see what I could learn before we fully stepped into the room and revealed ourselves. This situation could really get out of hand quickly if we weren't careful, and having the element of surprise was something I didn't want to give up just yet.

"What they've done or haven't done doesn't matter. This isn't your fight," Ramona snarled back at Angelo. "So, leave. Fifi already fired you anyway, so you have no business here. Go, run and hide to Mommy and Daddy's mansion."

"I'm not leaving," he said, his eyes starting to burn red as his skin deepened a few shades. He was seconds away from taking on his incubus form and that wouldn't be pretty. But, if Ramona took on her wraith form, that wouldn't be pretty either.

"Fine, then you can die, just like your sister is going to," Ramona said, her voice deepening into something that sounded like a monster from a horror film. As I watched her, she started to glow a sickly green.

"What the hell are you talking about?" Angelo demanded, as his inky black and rubber-like wings shot out of his back, flapping a few times. The gnomes gasped and ran a few feet further behind him, clearly afraid of him, just as they should have been. An incubus in his demonic form was a scary sight to behold.

Ramona laughed, and the sound made me shiver because the tone was so deep and maniacal. It no longer sounded like the voice of a woman. "Are you really so blind?"

"I guess so," Angelo answered, while his eyes went from red to pitch black and his skin fully morphed into the leathery red of the incubus. I could feel my own succubus stirring within me, wanting to go to his aid. It was a built in response, but I was fairly sure I didn't possess the strength to fully transform.

"For what she did to Ophelia!" Ramona nearly spat.

"Wanda killed Ophelia," Angelo corrected her.

Ramona nodded. "They were in on it together," Ramona insisted. "And Wanda is next on my list."

"Why do you give two shits that Ophelia's dead?" Angelo continued, shaking his head. "Her death was a blessing to anyone who knew her."

With Ramona's back to us, I couldn't see her response, but I watched as her entire being shook and I imagined she was shaking with outrage. She began to lift off the ground, the ethereal green of her body doubling in brightness. And then the smell started to waft off her —the smell of death, the same scent I'd witnessed in the graveyard the night of Darragh and Cranough's murders, the same odor that had lingered outside the Broomstick Diner the night Angelo had confronted her. And now I had to wonder if he'd known the truth of what was really going on all along. He must have because he'd known about Darragh's death.

Because he was stalking you, I thought. *And good thing too, otherwise he never would have known the truth about Ramona.*

For a split second, I wondered if Angelo had been working with Ramona, but then I pushed that thought aside because it didn't fit with the situation unfolding in front of me now. Angelo had seemed legitimately surprised that Ramona wanted me dead.

"When my great-uncle married Ophelia, she became my family," Ramona explained.

"Oh, shit," I whispered, having never really understood why Ramona and Ophelia were close.

"Ophelia had agreed to leave Hallowed Realty to me if anything ever happened to her," Ramona continued, a hiss in her tone. "Instead, Wanda and Fifi dispatched her before she had a chance to write a proper will, which would have solidified my entitlement—and I was truly the person who should have benefitted from Ophelia's death, not your bimbo sister!"

Ramona took a deep breath and rose higher into the air, her glow increasing along with the horrific odor of rotting flesh. "I just want what's mine!"

"And you'd resort to murder to accomplish that?" Angelo asked, not appearing concerned in the least that she was taking her wraith form. Truly, there didn't seem to be much that intimidated him. In fact, I'd never seen him afraid before.

"I will relish Fifi's death!" Ramona yelled back as my heart started to pound.

"She's not going to touch a hair on your head," Taliyah whispered and started to move forward, but I held her back.

"You can't go after her, not when she's in her astral form and you're... basically human."

Taliyah paused. "What if I shoot her?"

"It won't do any good—the bullets would just go through her. She's basically a ghost—but an extremely dangerous and powerful one." Now taking on her wraith form, Ramona would be able to move through solid creatures and objects easily, stealing their life essence—just like Ophelia did when she neared a plant and it withered and died.

"No one lays a finger on my sister!" Angelo yelled, exploding into a burst of flames as he materialized directly in front of her, lunging at her. The gnomes behind him fled in every direction, shrieking.

A deep laugh echoed from Ramona as she easily outmaneuvered him, her ethereal form simply swaying out of the way, as if caught by the wind. "We both know you hate your sister as much as I do."

"That's where you're wrong." His skin darkened into a deep wine red and horns protruded from his skull. I couldn't remember the last time I'd seen my brother take his demon form but it was something to behold. "I don't hate my sister and I will protect her to the last."

Despite the horrible situation unfolding in front of me, I was struck by Angelo's words. And the fact that he actually cared about me. It was a feeling that not only shocked me, but warmed me at the same time.

In only a few seconds, Ramona's eerie green glow deadened and in its place was a fog of shadow and darkness—the true form of the wraith. As she flitted around, I was able to make out the white glow of her eyes. Other than that, her features were impossible to decipher, swallowed as they were by the shadow of her form. She screamed, filling the room with a terrifying, ear-splitting sound that brought both me and Angelo to our knees. Taliyah didn't seem to be affected by it in the same way.

Angelo yelled out in pain as Ramona flitted past him and as soon as she did, I watched numerous gashes appear along his cheeks, chin and forehead, as if she'd reached out and grated him with her clawed fingernails. Blood started to weep from his wounds.

"Angelo!" I yelled.

At the sound of my scream, Ramona jerked around in my direction, evidenced by her glowing white eyes which were now focused on me. She immediately floated towards me, but before she could reach me, Angelo materialized directly in front of me, appearing as a blaze of burning flames. Even though he was close to me, the fire from his form couldn't harm me, because it was the same fire that fueled my own succubus form.

However, it could hurt Taliyah and feeling the heat exiting him, she immediately crawled backwards, putting space between the two of them which was just as well.

"The only way we're going to be able to take her down is if she returns to her humanoid form," I whispered to him. He nodded so I faced Ramona, aware now of what we had to do. It was risky but I was also out of options.

"This issue is between the two of us, Ramona," I yelled as I took a step nearer her. "Leave Angelo out of it."

"*He* attacked me," Ramona responded, her voice sounding like a groan on the wind.

"And he's willing to return to his humanoid form, if you're willing to return to yours," I called back. "If so, I won't take on my succubus form, because if I do, you must realize you'll be outnumbered."

Ramona laughed, and it looked like a cloud of dark smoke coughing. "Outnumbered?" She ridiculed me. "I know you lack the sustenance required to take on the form of the succubus."

"That's where you're wrong," I lied. "I've been feeding from Roy and I possess the necessary strength, but I want to deal with this situation woman to woman." I could only hope she believed me, because if she didn't, she'd realize she could definitely take on Angelo and me, because we weren't as powerful as she was.

She paused for a moment, not responding, just floating there like a dark cloud. A dark and very stinky cloud.

"Woman to woman, I'm more powerful than you are," she said.

I nodded. "Then the fight will be in your favor."

I could only assume she didn't detect Taliyah, who was still on all fours behind Angelo and waiting in the shadows, her weapon drawn. Ramona swooped upward and emitted another blood-curdling scream, and that was when I realized she had no plans to return to her corporeal form. And why would she? She was much stronger in her wraith form.

I reached inside my pocket and produced the black Sharpie I'd shoved in it before I'd jumped into Taliya's police vehicle. The Sharpie had been magicked by Wanda, enchanted with sigils and wards that would allow me to draw a circle on the ground that would act as a cage to any supernatural creature. It was the supernatural answer to Mace essentially, and Wanda sold the bewitched pens at her store.

Noticing Angelo was further away from Ramona than I currently was, I threw the Sharpie to him.

"Draw a circle on the ground!" I yelled in our native tongue so Ramona wouldn't understand me.

The magical sigils used to create the cage would render Ramona motionless and solid long enough for us to force her back into her corporeal form. Angelo, disappeared in a flurry of red-orange flames, grabbed the Sharpie from midair, then dropped down to his knees and immediately started drawing a large circle—big enough that Ramona could fit into it. Meanwhile, I faced Ramona squarely, intent on keeping her attention.

"You killed Cranough, Darragh and Saffron!" I yelled at her.

Ramona laughed. "And it took you way too long to figure out."

She jerked toward me and her eyes burned bright white in the midst of the darkness of her shadowy form. I turned and ran, forcing her to give chase. She was fast, and I knew I'd tire quickly, especially since I wasn't in my full succubus form and hadn't fed recently enough. But, I needed to buy as much time for Angelo as I could.

I glanced back at him and noticed he was finished drawing the circle so I reversed direction and started running towards him. Ramona was right behind me, apparently oblivious to the outline of the cage on the floor. I ran across the sigils, fully aware they were harmless to me, since I was the owner of the Sharpie, but the moment Ramona drifted across them, the sigils activated, sending shocks of blue light straight upward. The blue lights acted like ethereal prison bars and immediately locked her in.

As soon as she was imprisoned in the magical holding cell, the wards forced her back into her humanoid shape. She let out one final piercing scream as the fog of her shadow started to circle rapidly within the cage, little by little taking on the shape of a woman—a naked and old one.

Once Ramona completed the transition to her human form, Taliyah moved forward, yanking out a taser gun and tasing Ramona with it. Immediately, Ramona dropped to all fours as her body spasmed a few times, as if still trying to fight the inevitable, but soon she was out.

After that, I just stood there for a second, panting for breath, while I tried to talk myself out of passing out. I was exhausted—mentally and physically and the need to feed was almost overwhelming.

With a great swoosh of his wings, Angelo landed beside me and his wings rescinded into his back while his skin began to blanch into its customary olive. The horns in his forehead sunk back into his skull and fairly soon, he was facing me with a smile, standing completely naked.

"That sigil cage was good thinking, sister," he said with a broad smile.

Even naked as he was, I didn't waste any time in throwing my arms around him. I just was so happy to see him basically unharmed (minus the gashes Ramona had left in his face). I was about to say as much when Taliyah walked over to the glowing blue cage which held the now unconscious Ramona. She took one look at Ramona and then turned to face us as I released Angelo and he gave Taliyah a big grin.

"Can't you supernaturals remember to bring a change of clothing with you?" Taliyah asked, frowning at Angelo who did nothing but stand there with his legs wide and his hands on his hips. He was and always had been proud of his naked body. She cocked one eyebrow and then stared pointedly at his manhood, as if to say she wasn't impressed.

I couldn't help my laugh.

"And where would be the fun in that?" Angelo responded to her with an added wink, clearly flirting. And his flirting with Taliyah made sense because she was a beautiful woman

Meanwhile, the gnomes peeked out from behind various doors leading from the large lobby. Slowly, they began to venture back out into the open.

"It's safe," I called out, and they came further into the room. Then I turned to face Taliyah. "What are you going to do with her?" I asked, motioning to Ramona's still body. "It's not as though you can put her in a normal jail cell. Once the effects of the cage wear off, she could and probably will return to her wraith form and then you won't be able to hold her."

Before she could answer, a car pulled up in front of the building and all three of us turned to see Fox and Roy stepping out of a large, black towncar that must have, no doubt, belonged to Fox. At the realization that Fox was now here... with Taliyah, I swallowed hard.

But, then I remembered Fox wouldn't recognize Taliyah because she'd been essentially in protection with her human family from the time she was a child. And of course she'd have no clue who Fox was because she'd never met him before.

"Fifi, are you okay?" Roy asked as he walked through the door and immediately threw his arms around me, holding me tight. A second or so later, he released me from his bear hug and wrapping his hands around my arms, held me at arm's length as he inspected me.

"I'm fine," I answered. It took another five minutes or so for me to explain everything that had just happened, which led us right back to the same question I'd just asked Taliyah—what were we going to do with Ramona?

"I'll take her," Fox said. "I know a hunter with the facilities to hold a creature of her ilk."

"Are you sure?" Taliyah asked as she faced her future husband. Both of them just stood there, looking at each other with what appeared to be confused interest— as if they somehow recognized one another but weren't sure how or why.

"I'm positive," Fox replied, taking her hand. "We have yet to meet."

"I'm the Chief of Police of Haven Hollow," she answered as she then cleared her throat and appeared uncomfortable. "But, you can... call me Taliyah."

"I'm Fox Aspen," he returned and then leaning down, kissed her hand. She just looked at him, surprise registering on her face, but she didn't pull away— something I found interesting because I didn't imagine she would have allowed anyone this type of liberty. Taliyah just had this independent, trust-no-one sort of attitude.

Fox smiled broadly at her and then turned around as he approached the cage that held Ramona. Taking out an eraser from his pocket, he began erasing the lines of the Sharpie. Clearly, the eraser was enchanted in order to be able to erase the Sharpie lines, not to mention the wards themselves. Once Fox finished, he took hold of Ramona's arm and crouching low, yanked her above his shoulder, and then stood up again.

Taliyah looked at him with curiosity, a flush spreading across her cheeks, along with confusion. He nodded to her and a moment later, disappeared in a flash of red-gold light. She just stood there, looking at the fading color in a daze before finally turning back to face the rest of us.

"So, how do we get justice for the grim and the elf?" she asked. "Since that... that *man* just absconded with the perpetrator."

I cocked my head the side as I considered it. "I think we just got justice for them. Fox will hand Ramona a life behind bars and she won't be a threat to Haven Hollow ever again."

"I would say I'd close the case, but I guess it was never really opened from an official standpoint," Taliyah answered, shrugging. "What should I do with the body of Cranough?"

"I'll have Bea get in contact with the Autumn Court," I answered, although I imagined Fox would beat us to it. No doubt, he'd want the body of Cranough returned to its rightful court anyway and I had a feeling he'd probably want to see Taliyah again—there had just been something there in his eyes when he'd looked at her. Maybe it was fate? Or maybe it was just another example of the undying romantic within me imagining things that weren't there.

Taliyah nodded. "I guess we're done here then."

"Looks that way," I replied, finally sighing a breath of relief as I faced my brother and... smiled.

Chapter Twenty-Three

"Are you okay?" I asked Angelo as he walked into my office. It had been an hour or so since Fox had removed Ramona and then disappeared. Afterwards, everyone had gone their merry way, and I'd told Angelo to meet me at Hallowed Homes. He and I needed to have a conversation.

When Angelo arrived, I had a first aid kit already laid out on my desk. "Sit down and let me clean up those wounds on your face."

"I'm fine."

"You may think you're fine but you look like crap."

Ramona's tears weren't the only inky thing about her. Everywhere she'd scratched or touched Angelo in her wraith form, her inky black residue was left behind. The longer the stuff sat on his skin or inside the wounds from her claws, the more it would seep into his body, eventually polluting his bloodstream. Not that much would come of that pollution—his incubus blood cells would reject her contamination, but he could still suffer a lowered immune system.

He groaned and sat down on top of my desk to let

me tend to his injuries as he winced and grumbled with each touch. "You're such a baby," I teased.

"A baby with hopefully a new commission," he said, smirking.

"You don't work here," I reminded him, my eyebrows reaching for the ceiling. "I fired you, remember? And, last I checked, you haven't been rehired." I pressed harder on one of his gashes than I needed to, but I smiled all the same. He had this coming to him, regardless of the fact that he'd come to my defense.

"Even after today?" He asked, wincing. "You'd still deny your favorite brother a job after he took on a wraith for you?"

"My *only* brother," I corrected him. "Besides, have you forgotten *why* I fired you?"

"For faulty reasons," he responded with a shrug. "You fired me over a lie you were told by the same wraith that just tried to kill us and our clients."

I looked at him as the pieces started to fall into place. Ramona had been lying about what had happened between them—when she'd said he'd demanded sexual favors from her. Truly, she'd just wanted to get him out of the way and thanks to Angelo's habit of being a 24/7 jerk, she knew it wouldn't be hard to convince me that he'd attempted to intimidate her. That part I understood, but there was still one piece to the puzzle that was missing.

"So that night at the Broomstick Diner," I started as I moved to the next gash on his face and dousing the cotton ball with rubbing alcohol, set to cleaning the wound as he continued to wince. "When I caught you yelling at Ramona."

"What of it?"

"What were the two of you arguing about?"

"You," he answered with a shrug.

"Me?"

He nodded and then further explained. Apparently Ramona's plan where I was concerned was to first ruin Hallowed Homes, so she killed Darragh and Cranough, hoping their deaths would start to destroy Hallowed Homes' reputation. And then she'd frightened Saffron to death after her interview, in order to ensure I didn't hire anyone new.

The gnomes had been next on her list. Only this time, she'd planned to get me involved. She'd intended to lure me to the golf course, telling me the gnomes were encountering some type of problem with the property. When I arrived to help, she was going to murder me, after having already done away with all the gnomes. And then she intended to frame me for the deaths of Darragh, Cranough, Saffron and the gnomes, blaming it on the fact that because I hadn't been feeding properly, my hunger finally got the best of me, and I went AWOL, attacking as many creatures as I could. Because I'd be dead, I wouldn't be able to defend myself. And she didn't imagine Angelo would defend me, since all he wanted was to ruin me anyway.

"But why did Ramona tell you all this?" I asked, shaking my head.

Angelo shrugged. "She misjudged our sibling animosity and believed I hated you, so she figured I'd want in, that I'd help her with her plan." He cocked his head to the side as he looked at me. "And of course I played along with her for a while, so I could understand just exactly what she was planning."

"And the argument that happened between the two of you the night I saw you with her at the Broomstick?"

"I told her the plan had too many holes in it and that

I wouldn't have anything to do with it. Of course, that infuriated her, and when I told her she'd better abandon the plan altogether or I'd alert the authorities, she further refused so... I lost my temper."

"Hmm," I answered, chewing on my lower lip as I recalled Angelo's anger that night. I'd never seen him so fired up before. "So why didn't you come to me to warn me about what Ramona was planning?"

He shrugged. "I planned to tell you, but then you fired me and pissed me off."

"I pissed you off enough that you were going to let Ramona kill me?" I asked, my mouth dropping open.

"No, of course not," he responded and shook his head like I was stupid for thinking so. "That's why I showed up at the gnome compound. I knew she was going to stick to her idiotic plan, so I came prepared to kill her before she could kill you or them."

I nodded and then took a deep breath as everything began to settle and I started to see my brother in a different light—a light I'd never before seen him in. "I'm sorry, Angelo."

He frowned up at me, appearing surprised. "For what?"

"For thinking that you were behind the murders."

He shrugged. "I mean... I guess I can see how you would have thought it was me."

"And I'm sorry for believing Ramona when she said you came onto her. I should have known better."

His frown grew more pronounced as his eyebrows met in the middle of his face and his eyes narrowed. "She said I came onto her?"

I nodded and explained the conversation that had occurred right after he'd left the Broomstick. All the while, the disgust on his face grew.

"Fifi, you really thought I would have demanded sexual favors from *her*?" he asked, frowning at me. "Don't you know me at all? Ugh, that's disgusting."

I laughed at his revulsion as I cleaned off the last of his wounds and began clearing away the cotton pads and alcohol into a small plastic bag. I would throw the bag into a fire later, because that was the only way to dispose of wraith contamination.

"So how do you think Ramona killed Darragh and Cranough?" I asked, before answering part of my own question. "Well, she killed Darragh with the *Spirit Bane* but where did she get it?"

Angelo shrugged. "The Underground Potions market is thriving, as you know. She could have gotten it from anyone. The point is that she did get it and that was how she killed Darragh."

"And Cranough and Saffron?"

"And I'm fairly sure she scared them both to death as wraiths are known to do," he answered on a shrug. "Just like she would have attempted with the two of us."

"Hmm."

"I'm not exactly sure, though, because we never got that far in our conversations. I guess you'll have to get that answer from Fox."

I nodded and then was quiet for a few seconds. "I really thought you hated me."

"Well, you aren't my favorite person sometimes and I hate the way you're running this place," he continued as he looked around and then shook his head. "But I wouldn't want you dead."

"You wouldn't?"

Much to my surprise, he reached up and smacked me lightly on the back of the head like he used to do when we were kids.

"I'm your brother, dummy. No, I don't want you dead."

I laughed and closed up the first aid kit, putting it away before sitting down at my desk to face him. We both just sat there for a moment, looking at one another. I was exhausted. Relieved, yes, but exhausted.

"I wouldn't want you dead either and I've never hated you," I said with a smile. "Just for the record."

"Good to know," he answered with a low chuckle.

"Okay, so," I started, needing to move on to the next topic. "Regarding your employment here."

"Am I still employed here?"

I laughed, enjoying the power I had over him—at least for the moment. "No, you know you aren't."

"Can I come back?"

"On one condition."

He frowned. If Angelo hated one thing, it was rules. Well, now he was about to get a whole bunch of them. "Which is?"

"You need to let me run this place the way *I* want to run it and stop trying to second guess me and constantly make me look bad in front of my employees."

"Ugh," he grumbled.

"I mean it, Angelo."

"Okay, what else?"

"You have to start seriously following my rules."

"And what rules are we talking about?"

"No ruining marriages and families," I started. "In fact, no seducing clients at all, that means no feeding off anyone you meet through Hallowed Homes. I'm introducing a strict no-business-mixed-with-pleasure rule."

"Ugh," he grumbled again.

"I mean it, Angelo," I warned him.

"What else?"

"No sabotaging me. Your previous behavior is part of the reason I believed Ramona when she told me you tried to seduce her."

He shrugged. "That's fair, I guess." Then he extended his hand. "Deal?"

"Deal," I answered as I shook it. "But, this is your last chance." He nodded, and we both were quiet for a few seconds before a smile took hold of my mouth. "I'm proud of you for doing what you did, Angelo," I started, needing him to hear these words even if he probably didn't want to hear them. In general, Angelo wasn't an emotional person. But, this was the first time he'd ever actually acted like a brother, and I wanted him to understand how much I appreciated it and him. "You finally became the big brother I always dreamed you could be."

He rolled his eyes and made a disgusted sound but I could tell he was happy by the big smirk that soon took control of his mouth. "Don't let it go to your head."

***

"Why would you go willingly into a dangerous situation like confronting Ramona without me?" Roy asked a few hours later. We were standing in his living room, facing each other, and he didn't look happy. Once Angelo left the office, Roy texted me to ask me to stop by and now here I was.

"I'm a big girl, Roy. I knew what I was doing, and I wanted to take care of the issue myself."

"And Taliyah?"

I nodded. "Well, including Taliyah, I guess."

"I'm still upset with you because you took a chance

you didn't need to," Roy said, nodding down at me. "I'm your friend and that's what friends do—they're there for each other and in my case, I protect you and I don't want that changing."

"Well, I appreciate that."

He nodded and then started pacing his living room floor, running his hands through his hair and appearing completely agitated. "You have no idea how worried I was!"

"I'm sorry."

"I had no idea where you were going and it was everything Fox could do to try to keep up with you! You were driving like a bat out of hell!"

"I didn't even realize you were following me."

"Yeah, because we could barely keep up!"

I just smiled at him and watched him continue to pace. Then, touched by his obvious concern for me, I walked up to him and took his hand, stopping him where he stood. "I'm sorry I didn't include you, Roy, but I appreciate everything you did in coming after me. And I appreciate your friendship more than you know."

As I held his hand, I noticed something interesting in the way he looked at me. There was just something in his eyes—something that seemed almost like... desire? It caused me to immediately reflect on the way Poppy had insisted she was fine with the idea of Roy and me dating. I couldn't explain why, but at that very moment, the idea didn't seem so... bizarre or so wrong.

I leaned up on my tip toes, about to tell him he didn't have to worry about me and that I could take care of myself, but before I could utter a word, his lips were on mine. I was slightly confused for a moment, because I didn't remember coming in for the kiss and, furthermore, I was pretty convinced Roy was only interested in my friendship. But, no, we were kissing and he'd definitely been the one who initiated it and...

Will you stop overthinking and just enjoy this! The succubus yelled at me.

I'm not sure how long it was that we kissed, but in that lip-lock, I could feel the succubus drawing his life energy and it felt... incredible. When we finally pulled away, I immediately opened my mouth to apologize, somehow worried that I was again at fault for what had just happened. But, before I could say anything, he kissed me again. And this time, he didn't just kiss me. This time his hands were in my hair and his body was pressed up against mine. This time the kiss was... different to any other kiss we'd ever shared.

When he pulled away a few seconds later, I was speechless. Confused, baffled, excited, nervous...

"Dinner tomorrow night?" he asked, further shocking me.

I didn't understand what was going on. How was it that we'd just gone from friends to... kissing to... him asking me out on a date? Was he even asking me out on a date or maybe he was just asking me to dinner... as friends? Hmm, I wasn't sure. In fact, I had no idea what was going on.

"Um," I started, fully aware that only the other day he'd said he wasn't over Poppy. And, furthermore, there was still the promise I'd made to myself—that because Roy and I were very close friends, I wouldn't risk our friendship. Besides, my terrible luck with men was never far from my thoughts and I really didn't want to add Roy to my long list of failed relationships.

Whatever this kiss was, whatever these *kisses* were, we could still write them off as brief moments of madness—just whims we both happened to give into.

"Um?" he repeated.

"Dinner… as friends?" I asked.

He seemed as confused as I was. "I don't know, Fifi."

"I don't know either… I mean, I don't understand what's going on between the two of us right now."

"I know we're friends," he started, but then shook his head. "But…"

I stepped away from him and when he attempted to pull me back into the heat of his embrace, I held one hand out to keep him where he was. "Let's not mess this up."

He frowned. "What does that mean?"

"It means… we're good as friends, Roy, so let's just… keep it at that."

He nodded and gave me an understanding smile. "Let's still do dinner tomorrow night, I mean… if you're free… and it'll be a non-date."

I grinned. "A non-date it is."

The End

To be continued in:
All Hallows Eve
Haven Hollow #10
by J.R. Rain &
H.P. Mallory
Coming soon!

About J.R. Rain

J.R. Rain is the international bestselling author of over seventy novels, including his popular Samantha Moon and Jim Knighthorse series. His books are published in five languages in twelve countries, and he has sold more than 3 million copies worldwide.

Please find him at: www.jrrain.com.

About H.P. Mallory

H.P. Mallory is a New York Times and USA Today bestselling author. She has eleven series currently and she writes paranormal fiction, heavy on the romance! H.P. lives in Southern California with her son and a cranky cat.

To learn more about H.P. and to download free books, visit: www.hpmallory.com

J.R. RAIN AND H.P. MALLORY